D1525596

For Love For Freedom

© Copyright Richard Riemer 2022
Published by Glorybound Publishing
SAN 256-4564
1st Edition
Published in the United States of America
KDP ISBN 9798419868465
Copyright data is available on file.
Remer, Richard, 1950-
    For Love For Freedom/Richard Riemer
        Includes biographical reference.
1. Fiction   2. Historical Fiction
I. Title

www.gloryboundpublishing.com

Acknowledgment and disclosure,

This story is historical fiction. Any references to historical events, real people, or real places may be used fictitiously. Names, characters, dates and places may be products of the author's imagination and are created for the entertainment of the audience. Unless otherwise noted, Photographs, maps, graphs, paintings and other images were available in the public domain on the Internet.

For Love
For
Freedom

by Richard Riemer

Glorybound Publishing
Camp Verde, Arizona
in the year 2022

Dedication

This book is dedicated to,

Johann and Sophia Kemp

Preface

In 2016, Dr. Nina Look, who was at the time, Senior Archivist at the Ozaukee County Historical Society, in Cedarburg, Wisconsin, introduced me to my great-great-great grandparents, Johann and Sophia Kemp.

Her discovery launched an all-consuming five-year study by me, of these two extraordinary individuals and their descendants. She discovered where Johann and Sophia were born and where they lived in 1829. I learned that they lived in Mecklenburg, and the likely reasons why they chose to leave.

The ship that they traveled on and the port of entry that they arrived at in America is a matter of record. Their route between Baltimore and Milwaukee is the trail most all immigrants traveled on from Baltimore to Wisconsin Territory in 1829. Johann and Sophia's incredible love story is wondrous.

Table of Contents

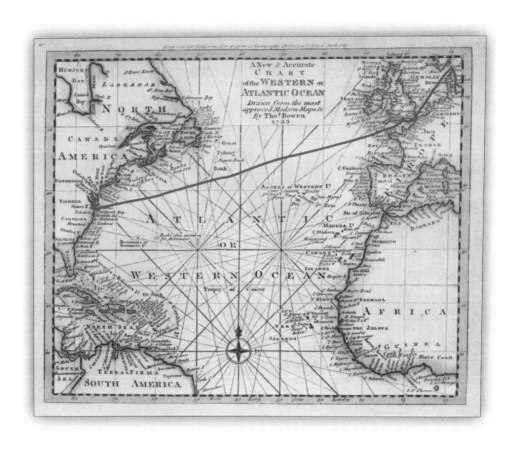

Johann and Sophia's Atlantic crossing from
Mecklenburg to Baltimore, Maryland, USA.

Johann and Sophia's overland journey from
Baltimore, Maryland to Milwaukee.

Chapter One

A Type of Feudalism

Surviving through the day is my first thought every morning and will be my last thought every night. Do I have enough food? Will I have a safe place to stay tonight? There is little time to think of anything else. The year is 1828. I'm sixteen years old and I reside in rural Mecklenburg. I live with my father, mother, younger sister Anna, and my grandparents. I have two older brothers, but I haven't seen them in years. Mother and father fear that they have died. You see, during the years of Napoleonic occupation of our country my brothers, Dietrich and Otto were drafted into the French army to battle the Russians. They were such an impressive sight as they marched away in cadence with the French troops.

That was four years ago. Oh, how I wanted to go with them, as I cheered and waved with the crowd. I was sure that they would soon be marching home, victorious with medals pinned on their chests. When I turned to my father, Petrus, and mother, Maria, there were tears in their eyes as they quietly waved goodbye to their sons. That was the last time I saw my brothers. I still think of them every day. My mother and father, well, they haven't been the same since the day their sons marched off to war. I worry that they never will be.

My family and I live a life of servitude, working the land for Baron von Gutenriemer. In our country, there is a type of feudalism known as "inherited serfdom". The noblemen, such as Baron von Gutenriemer control the political power and rule their massive estates with absolute authority. As serfs, we are assets of the property, in kind with the cattle and poultry. We are dependent on the noblemen, and landowners for every part of our lives. My family and I have no rights of any kind. It's the way we have lived our entire lives. I live as my father had, and his father before him. The baron's approval and permission are required for everything we do, including leaving the Baron's property or even getting married. Punishment is harsh and certain for disobeying the Baron's rules.

As many as 50,000 serfs work the Baron's land. In exchange for my family's service, working his land from dawn to dusk six days a week, we are provided a place to live. Our family, including my grandfather and grandmother, live in a 10' x 12' room in the laborer's cottage. We are allotted use of a one-half acre of land to grow food for our family. We are allowed to sell any produce that we grow in excess of our family's needs at the market in the nearby Village of Glashagen. My father is allowed to keep the proceeds to buy personal essentials.

Map of Germanic Kingdoms in 1828

This is the laborer's cottage where my family lives.

The area in the center of the cottage is a common space. It has a fireplace for all of the residents to cook our meals. In cold and stormy weather, we bring the livestock into the common space. It protects them and it also helps to keep the cottage warm in the winter.

My family and I live in a laborer's cottage
on Baron von Gutenriemer's property.

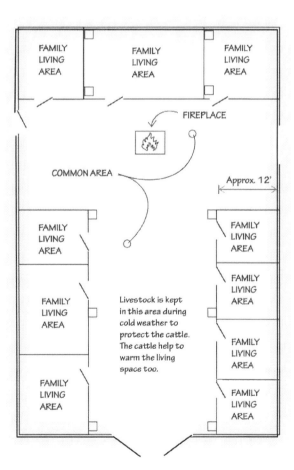

FAMILY LIVING AREA

FAMILY LIVING AREA

FAMILY LIVING AREA

FIREPLACE

COMMON AREA

Approx. 12'

FAMILY LIVING AREA

FAMILY LIVING AREA

FAMILY LIVING AREA

FAMILY LIVING AREA

Livestock is kept in this area during cold weather to protect the cattle. The cattle help to warm the living space too.

FAMILY LIVING AREA

FAMILY LIVING AREA

The House of Kemp

Left to right
Dietrich,
Otto,
Anna,
Father (Petrus)
Johann,
Mother, (Maria)

The House of Gutenriemer

Baron von Gutenriemer

Baroness von Gutenriemer
(died 1826)

Sophia Gwendolyn
Gutenriemer

Like most Mecklenburgers, we live in a rural area. Our family rarely is allowed to leave the Baron's compound, and when we do, it is to walk to Glashagen. It's about a mile north of us. There, we sell our produce, purchase items we need, and return right back home. In my lifetime I have never been anywhere beyond Glashagan, and I really haven't felt that I had a need to. I have no idea what the world is like beyond the Village of Glashagan.

For the first time in my memory, our little community of 70 people is hearing news from the outside world. There is talk of the 23 German-speaking kingdoms uniting into one nation! A radical concept indeed.

Here in Mecklenburg, we have been fortunate. Except for Napoleon's occupation of our country for three years, we have avoided most of the wars that have plagued the rest of the Germanic kingdoms. The Poles, Swedes, French, Russians, and Danes have all been invading the relatively small Germanic kingdoms. They are continually acquiring land around the perimeter of the Germanic countries. Some Kings and Dukes are talking about "unification for strength in unity."

An "enlightened absolutism" are also words that I am hearing a lot this year and it is now established in Prussia. I'm told that it's effects were being felt in many of the Germanic kingdoms and in our country as well. This new concept of the king being the "first servant of the state" is completely contrary to any government in Europe until now. In Prussia and Austria where this new concept is in practice, it has resulted in an increase in productivity and a flourishing economy. Now, legal reforms are taking place in Prussia, including the abolition of torture. Improvement in the status of Jews and Gypsies has been implemented in Prussia. They say that Austria has begun opening schools to educate the populous!

Prussian nobility is in high level talks about the emancipation of the serfs. Serfs are beginning to walk off of noblemen's properties and going to the villages. I sense that the noblemen are losing control over their serfs. My world is beginning to change, and it scares me a little bit. For the first time in my life, I don't know what tomorrow will bring.

Three weeks ago, I saw two men walking up the road. That was highly unusual for a work day. Last week there were two more men walking toward town, later that day a group of six men were walking north toward Glashagen. Today, there are many more peasants walking up the road. Some of the groups include women and children! It is the talk of my neighbors as we are working the fields. Who are they? Where are they going? We haven't seen anything like this before. The foreman who is mounted on his horse climbs down and is walking up to the picker's line with his whip and club. He is ordering us to keep working. I'm seeing peasants walking up the road all day today. Baron von Gutenriemer ordered that his serfs will not be allowed to leave the compound for any reason. His foreman for our labor group has been put on alert to be on the lookout for serfs that might try to leave his property.

The foreman called all the workers together today. We were told that anyone caught leaving the compound would be beaten. If anyone left the compound, and did not return, their family will be beaten. Tension is building and the foreman is doing a head count morning, noon, and night.

One of our neighbors talked to a person that was walking up the road. Our neighbor was told that Mecklenburg had made serfdom illegal last year and we didn't even know it until now. In the eyes of the law, we are free men. In the eyes of the Baron, we are still his property. He is still controlling our lives and we have no power to change that. The reality is, that everyone in our little community has been serfs for generations. It's all we know. I think that most of us have a fear of the world outside of our compound. The new laws that abolished serfdom also released the landowners from their obligation under feudal law to provide serfs housing and an opportunity to support themselves. I am now hearing stories of landholders putting the less productive, the elderly, and single women with children out on the street. To his credit, Baron von Gutenriemer has not done that to his serfs to my knowledge.

My father is a carpenter and builder for the Baron, and it puts him at a slightly higher status than field workers. He spends days working at the Baron's many properties. Now that I am sixteen years old, I will begin my apprenticeship working with my father in the carpenter trade. I have been looking forward to this day for so long. Today we are working at one of the baron's other labor compounds. In my life, I have never been to any compound other than ours. The buildings are laid out the same as ours in many ways.

Since I've been working with my father, time is flying by. It is the third week of my apprenticeship, and I am enjoying it completely. I love working with my father. Working with wood comes naturally to me. He said I am progressing well and that I will be a fine carpenter someday. Working as the Baron's carpenter apprentice has given me the opportunity to see some of his properties. Today is a special day, I will be working at the Baron's castle!

Today, I will be working at the baron's stable. It is quite magnificent with marble pillars, mahogany stalls, and running water. There are twenty stable attendants feeding, grooming and cleaning up after the horses. The Baron's horses are living in better conditions than my family is.

Gutenriemer Stables

I'm repairing horse stalls on my second day at the Baron's stable. It makes me proud to know that my father, Petrous Kemp, has earned the title of the Baron's Master Carpenter. I never knew this because my father is such a humble man. I am so proud to be his son.

The days are long when you work for the Baron. It's getting dark and the full moon is the only light to see. Someone is riding toward me on a white steed. It's the baron's daughter, Sophia, and she is wearing a red velvet dress. She is the most beautiful girl I have ever seen!

I have been working at the castle every day. It's been almost six weeks since I saw the Baron's daughter at the stable for that brief moment. I can't get her out of my mind! But I know my place in society. She was born into the temporal lords; a wealthy aristocratic class and I am just a lower-class laborer. The contrasts between us are insurmountable. She attended a private school. I don't know how to read or write. I must focus on my trade, work hard, and try to forget Sophia.

Because my father's craftsmanship has caught the attention of the Baron, we are spending most days working on the grounds of the Baron's main estate. Working this close to Baroness Sophia, makes it hard to forget her.

The state of our country is in complete disorder. Peasants are walking away from the landowner's property at will. They are starving in the villages. Robbery and muggings are rampant. I'm told there is rioting and looting all over Mecklenburg. Noblemen and peasants alike are blaming the King's leadership for the disorder.

Father and I smell smoke, so we run over to the front wall and up the steps to look over the castle wall. Shops and barns are ablaze in the village outside the gate. I hear trumpets sounding! I'm told by one of the guards that it is to call up the reserve guards that live in the village outside the gates.

I am concerned for my mother, sister, and grandparents. Are they safe at our home in the compound? Frankly, I'm beginning to be worried about my own life!

Angry crowds are walking toward us. The walls surrounding the castle are about forty feet high. So, except for dodging the occasional rock or brick that is thrown at me, I feel somewhat safe up here watching the events roll out. As I'm watching over the wall I'm thinking, "Although I don't know any of these people, from this distance they look just like the people that I've known all my life." Most of us peasants are kind and generous people, like my neighbors. If you were hungry, they would give you a meal even though they had very little to eat themselves. Now, these people below the wall are starving, and homeless, and they will kill to survive!

I can see the reserve guards that live in the village. They are wearing silver helmets and red vests like the castle guards that are next to me on the wall. The reserves are trying to come to the aid of the castle. The angry peasants outside aren't allowing them to approach the gate. I see some of the reserves are even taking off their uniforms and joining with the mob. Many of the men outside the wall are now carrying weapons such as axes, pitchforks, and clubs. The Captain of the Guards calls out, "they are trying to breach the gate!"

One of the Lieutenants orders the guards to begin boiling kettles of whale oil. Father explains to me, that when the oil gets to boiling temperature the castle guards will pour the scalding oil over the wall onto the peasants outside the gate below. I can only imagine how painful and disfiguring it must be for my countrymen below that will have the hot oil poured on them. I hope it doesn't come to that. Now, I hear the trumpeters sound to call up the marksmen. They come trotting up the steps to the wall overlooking the gate.

Peasants have begun ramming the gate with a log, trying to break it open. The gate is built of 12" thick beams and it is holding.

My father points at a larger battering ram that is being assembled at a distance that is out of range for the marksmen.

Up the stairs comes a tall man walking at a deliberate pace. He's wearing polished armor and a red cape that has the Gutenriemer crest on it. He's a handsome man with a well-trimmed beard that has a bit of gray under his chin. There is a lieutenant at his side and two guards behind him.

For many generations, the Gutenriemer family has successfully defended their estate from enemies with armies. In those cases, they had time to prepare for the attack. This attack by the peasants developed spontaneously. There is apparently no contingency plan to defend against this type of attack. Furthermore, the Baron and his generals seem to be incapable of creating a defense plan. Things are rapidly falling apart for the defense of the castle. I'm seeing fear and panic in the guards. Most of them have no experience in warfare at all.

The battering ram that they are building is now completed and the peasants are rolling it toward the castle gate. When they get in range the marksmen are ordered to fire on them. As the men that are pushing the ram are hit and fall, other peasants take their place. I had seen death before at our compound. It was common and almost always caused by disease. Last winter our neighbor Erma Schmidt and her baby died during child birth. Two years ago, when I was working with my cousin Emil, the plow horse that he was driving spooked and kicked him in the head. But I had never seen anyone kill another person. It's a sickening sight.

I see men outside the wall walking around with musket ball wounds. Others are laying down and dying from their wounds. As the battering ram approaches the gate, I hear one of the lieutenants call to the Baron saying that the oil is boiling and ready to be poured on the enemy. When I hear that I think to myself, the enemy? Those people aren't the enemy, they are our countrymen.

My father calls to me, "this is turning bad son! Follow me, we need to get the hell out of here, right now!" Father has been working at this castle for years and he knows every part of it. There are secret passages that only he and the Baron are aware of. I'm following him as he runs across the center court and to the back wing of the castle. There is a crashing sound behind us. It sounds like the front gate has been breached. I can hear cheering coming from outside the wall. I turn around to see that the Baron's guards and their officers are panicking and retreating.

Escape options for getting out of the castle alive are getting fewer by the second. Hundreds of peasants come rushing in. Discipline in the ranks of the castle guards has turned to panic. The officers are the first to cut and run. I turn and look up at the front wall. I don't see the Baron up there anymore and I won't speculate as to his fate. It's getting dark. The escape route that Father had hoped to take is locked. The stable is the one and only place that I know well on the property. "Father, come with me, to the stable, fast!" Although, I don't have a clue what to do when we get there. As I'm running, I'm thinking about my mother and sister. Are they safe? I must get to them. Before I open the door to the stable, I quickly look back. The castle is ablaze!

I swing the door to the stable open. It's completely dark inside. I remember that there were some torches in a box inside the door, on the right. I grab one and light it. Some of the peasants are coming this way. Father says, "quick get a horse, and let's get out of here!" It sounds like a good idea, except that, I have never ridden a horse before! I guess I'll have to learn how to tonight.

I run to one of the horse stalls and I swing open the gate to see that magnificent white steed that Sophia rides. I'm startled to see that there is someone hiding in the corner of the stall behind the horse. Panic overtakes me. He's in the shadow and I can't make him out. Quickly, I look around for something to defend myself with and I realize that I'm holding a thirty-inch torch in my hand. I hold the torch up and move it from side to side trying to get him out of the shadow so I can see him. In a demanding voice, I order, "come out into the light so I can see you!"

Darn it, that sounded like my scared squeaky voice. Wait a moment, is he a woman? Yes, he looks like a woman. It is a woman She's hiding her face in her hands. "Come out of there" I demand.

"Stand up and come out!" She slowly stands up with her head down.

"Do you have a weapon? Let me see your hands and your face!" I command.

 She hesitates for a moment and then looks up at me. I raise my torch over her face to reveal the most beautiful woman I have ever seen in my life! It's the Baroness Sophia Gwendolyn Gutenriemer. I am humbled to be in her presence. I take off my hat and tip my head down. Then I drop to one knee. I'm not really sure if it's what I'm supposed to do, but is the first thing that comes to mind, so I do it.

I can hear angry voices. They're getting closer.

"An angry mob is coming. We are in danger if we stay here, Baroness, please, we must leave now your highness." Father pleads in a respectful tone of voice.

The Baroness pauses for a moment as she listens to the crowd in the courtyard, then turns to me and commands in a loud voice, "saddle my horse, peasant."

"Yes, Milady" I quickly respond.

I have never saddled a horse before. But I've watched the Baron's hostlers saddle and bridle horses while I was working in the stable. I think I can do it. I run to the tack room and can see that the Baroness' saddle and harness are clearly marked. I grab them along with a saddle pad run back to her horse. The baroness snatches the saddle pad out of my hand and throws it over her horse. As I begin putting the saddle on her horse, the Baroness grabs it from me.

"Get out of my way peasant," she commands. After she puts the saddle on, I hand her the harness. By this time Father has his horse saddled and bridled, He has picked one for me, and is just finishing cinching the saddle. The Baroness is not waiting. Just as I finish buckling her saddle she is on her horse and out the door at a brisk gallop. Father follows her. I climb on my horse, and he follows them without command. I'm just holding on. Father and I are at a full run, trying to keep up with the Baroness.

Looking back over my shoulder I see the castle ablaze. My thoughts are for the Baroness. She has lost her father, mother, and everything that she has ever known as home. Sophia keeps riding without looking back at the burning castle. Something is telling me that she will never look back and that she has already moved on to her new life.

We have been riding for about an hour. We are trying to find sanctuary, but the danger is everywhere. The horses are tired. The Baroness sees a bridge, and pulls off the road. We go under it to rest and water the horses. This is the first time since we escaped the castle that we have stopped. I must say, I'm too intimidated in the presence of the Baroness to say anything, so I think that I'll stay quiet and let someone else talk first.

After a few minutes of uneasy silence Father says, "Baroness, Johann and I are going to the compound where we live to check on our family. It is our duty to protect you, Your Highness, and we invite you to come with us." The Baroness is not accustomed to having a serf telling her what they are going to do, and she let Father know it. But she doesn't have a better plan, so she agrees to come along with us.

*The Peasant revolution has spread throughout all of the Germanic countries. More than 300,000 peasants revolted. Tens of thousands of peasants have already died fighting for their cause. As many as one hundred thousand will die before it was over. ***

It is early dawn when we reach our compound. There is a dense fog on the ground, so we are riding into the compound at a cautious pace. It's quiet, too quiet. There should be voices. I don't hear the cattle or poultry. Petrus gives his horse a gentle kick with his heels. His horse responds with a trot to the cottage door. I follow. He quickly hops off his horse and hurries in the door and runs to our room. No one is home. The place was torn apart! I run to the room next door calling, "Mutter! Anna!" No one is there either! Where is everyone?

* google.com

29

I run out of the room to the common area calling out, "Mutter! Anna! Mutter!" No response; "Grovotter! Grobmutter!"

Again, no answer. I look in the next-door neighbor's room and see two strange men inside. I ask; "Ver bis du? Wo sind die Schmitz?" (Who are you? Where are the Schmitz?)

They reach for their weapons, so I back out of the door, then turn and run. Father reaches for a sickle, and I grab a scythe. The men are standing at the door and don't pursue me. Father and I continued to run around the compound looking for our family. They are not to be found and neither are our neighbors. We can't find anyone that we know in the compound, but we do get the attention of a few dozen squatters that had moved in. They're talking about the Baroness, who is with our horses. She is kind of a standout in this crowd with her black velvet cape, pearl embroidered red velvet dress, and her soft, clean face and hands.

"There is nothing for us here," father says as he mounts his horse, "we will be in danger if we stay. We must leave now My Lady."

The Baroness is standing next to her mount and looking at me. With a demanding voice, she says, "well aren't you going to help me up on my horse, peasant?"

I know that the Baroness is an excellent equestrian. When I saw the stable hands offer to assist her assistance in mounting her horse, she had always refused. I think to myself; "how do I do this?"

I feel sweat forming on my forehead, and I know that my ears are turning red as people tell me they do in situations like this. I know, I'll hold her by the waist and kind of lift her up.

"Careful Johann, don't touch her butt." Here I go, take-off, and she is up in the saddle. Nothing to it. Although she did all the work. The Baroness looks over her shoulder with a flirtatious smile, she spurs her horse and gallops away.

My Father is now riding at the lead. He's decided that we should check out another one of the Baron's nearby labor communes. Father knows many of the people who live there. It may be a safe place to go until we have a plan as to what we want to do going forward. With Father at the lead, we cautiously approach the compound. There are lookouts at the entrance and one of them recognizes my father and allows us to pass. Groups from other labor compounds have already joined this compound. It appears that there are at least two hundred and fifty peasants here and the numbers are growing.

The Baroness is getting angry looks from the people around her. Father tells her, "You may be overdressed for this occasion, My Lady. Might I suggest changing into something a bit more appropriate for these times? If you like I will trade your cape and dress for attire that blends a bit better with the crowd."

As grotesque as that sounds to the Baroness, she reluctantly agrees. The baroness rubs a little dirt on her hands and face, lets her hair down and she blends fittingly. Now she has to remember not to speak. Good luck with that.

"Let's find mother." I say. Father went one direction; The Baroness and I go the other. As we are walking, I'm telling her that my dream in life is to own my own land and grow my own crops. Most of the land in Mecklenburg belongs to the aristocratic class. It is impossible for the lower class to own land.

The Baroness speaks. "Go to America. I have been told that land is quite plentiful, and it is inexpensive."

I reply, "what is America? Where is America? I will go to America, and I will buy land!"

Our conversation continues. The Baroness is openly telling me how she despised her circumstances.

"Living in the castle is like living in a prison with guards around me constantly. Their job is to protect me and keep me within the castle walls. I've had no normal childhood as you know it."

She's explaining how she spent her time looking out the window with envy watching the children outside the walls having fun. She is telling me that until this moment she never had anyone that she felt she could trust to speak to openly and honestly.

She confesses, "My mother died when I was ten years old. I truly believe that my father and his dominant ways contributed to her death." She goes on to say, "The only time I have felt free is when I'm riding my horse, Flossy."

She tells me that she hates her father for putting her in the position she is in. The Baroness goes on to say that there is no love in her family like the love that she sees in families that are outside the castle walls. She's telling me that she sees the love and devotion in mine, and is admittedly envious of me.

Father comes running saying, "Johann, I found them in one of the barns. Come quick!"

We run over to the barn and then go inside to my family I am so happy to see them! I give my mother, Anna, and Grandmother a hug. Grandfather is lying on the hay face up, expressionless, and in a comatose state.

I turn my head to Mother and before I can ask, she says, "He has the fever. He has been lying there like this since we arrived here. I'm so worried."

I walk over to Grandfather and kneel next to him. I hold his hand. It's as cold. His breath is shallow and irregular.

I lean over him and whisper into his ear, "Grubvater bitte nicht sterben." (Grandfather please don't die.) With tears in my eyes, I kiss him on his forehead.

The Baroness is standing at a distance watching us and thinking, how wonderful it must be to have a family that loves each other the way these people do.

Later in the evening, the Baroness and I talk to Father about going to America. After a lengthy discussion about all of our options, it seems that we convinced him that the best way to protect his family from the danger in Europe is to escape to America. Father confesses that he has been considering moving our family to America for some time now. He learned that the only way that he can afford to take his family to America is on a cargo clipper ship and travel in steerage. Father tells us that there are two seaports in Mecklenburg that accommodate international shipping. They are the Port of Hamburg and the Port of Grob Klein. Hamburg is about seventy miles farther away so we will of course go to Grob Klein.

Father says, "We will use the horses as pack horses. It will take two days to get there. We will leave in the morning."

As my family and I are leaving the compound. I see a man who catches my eye. He stands out in the crowd in that he's tall with a straight posture. His clothing is that of any peasant, but he has a groomed beard with just a spot of gray at his chin. I walk by him and then pick up my pace to catch up with the others. The Baroness is talking to me as we walk, although I'm not listening to her. All I can think of is the man with the gray patch on his beard. There were two other men with him too. That's right, I remember now! Could that have been Baron von Gutenriemer?

The Baroness continues talking but I'm not hearing a word that she's saying. The man had a clean complexion.

He's clearly not like any peasant that I've known. The Baroness punches me in the arm in a playful way and says, "You haven't heard a word that I've said, have you?"

I respond, "Of course I have."

As we continue walking, I smile and pull my shoulder away a bit in anticipation of another playful punch. I hear her flirtatious laugh I think that it is an indication that I'm not in trouble with her. We continue walking and she begins talking again. I'm hearing her talk but I'm not listening to what she's saying. All I can think about is how it makes me happy just having her walking next to me. I have never experienced anything like this before in my life.

Grandfather passed away in the night while I was sleeping. This is the saddest day of my life. I loved him so much. He was my other father to me. I can't imagine how my life will be without him. Tears are running down my face and I can't control them. I don't want to let the Baroness see me crying so I turn away from her. The Baroness sees me standing next to Grandfather and she walks over to me and gently hugs me around my shoulders. It's the first time that she has touched me. Except for punching me in the shoulder. I sense that she has never before felt close enough to anyone to be able to hug them.

Chapter Two

Tell Me About This America

Father is a clever man. He knows that to convince Mother and Grandmother to do something, he needs to have it be their idea. And, he has perfected the process of doing it over the years.

Father calls our family together for a meeting and says, "We can't stay here. The food reserves have run out and it is becoming dangerous. We must decide on our next move."

I watch as everyone looks around at each other waiting for someone to speak.

Mother is the first to speak. She asks, "Can we go to a different country where there is no peasant revolt?"

Again, we all look around at each other in silence...

My father looks at me and I know that it's my cue to speak. I look at the Baroness and say, "tell me again about this America of which you speak. Is it true that there are vast amounts of inexpensive land to be had? Is it true that there are all the freedoms that you told me about? Are the peasants revolting there too? Tell us where is this America?"

I look at Mother and Anna. It's obvious to me that they had never heard of such a place by the way they were looking at me. I'm sure that they are thinking that there is no such place in the world.

Anna speaks up. "Fee schwanz. (fairy tale) You are dreaming again Johann. There is no such place as this America that you are talking about. Now be serious."

She looks at Father seeking agreement. Father is looking at the Baroness and says, "Tell us, my Lady. Tell us about America."

Anna rolls her eyes up, frowns, then faces Father, "She has nothing to say here Father. She is not part of our family."

Father is still facing the Baroness. "Please speak My Lady, please tell us about America. Are there opportunities that I have heard about?"

The Baroness pauses as she chooses her words, leans forward slightly, and says, "My mentors have told me of a place that is across the ocean called America. It's a vast country where common men can own and work their own land. It's a place where every man can vote to choose their leaders. It's a country where every citizen has the right to disagree and speak out about their leaders without fear of persecution."

Mother looks at Grandmother and then at Father and speaks. "I say we go to America. What do you think?"

After quietly listening to the conversation, Grandmother speaks up and says to Father. "We will go to America. We will leave now."

We load the pack horses, and we are on our way. I expect our trip to America will be perilous. The Baroness seems as happy as I am, just to be together. Occasionally, she will punch me in the arm in a playful way and giggle. Father and Mother seem to approve of my new friend. I feel that they have concerns over whether there can be any long-term relationship between two people that have come from such extremely different backgrounds. I hope that I have their support though. They just don't want me to be hurt. Anna, well Anna does not like the Baroness at all. You see, Anna and I have been best friends from birth. For as long as I can remember we always wanted to be together. We love each other as siblings and best friends. I think Anna is feeling betrayed. She sees the Baroness taking her place in my life and feels helpless to do anything about it.

It just hit me. The tall man dressed as a peasant that I saw in the crowd is Baron von Gutenriemer! He miraculously survived the attack on his castle! The Baron is hated by many of the lower classes that he ruled. Dressed as a peasant he hopes to avoid confrontation with his enemies. I hope that he didn't see the Baroness. Certainly, she didn't see her father. I would know if she did. As the Baroness explained it to me. The Baron has no real love for his daughter. He thinks of her as his property, and he did not want anyone to have her except himself. He would go as far as having anyone killed who would take her away. I make a pledge to myself today. "I will protect her with my life."

I am worried about Grandmother. She is morning the sudden loss of her lifelong partner. She had been with Grandfather since she was fifteen years old. Grandmother has eaten only a half cup of rabbit stew since grandfather died. She is now unable to walk. Father orders us to stop and rest. While we are stopped, he makes a travois sled to pull behind one of the horses so that Grandmother can lay down in it. Father lays her down in the sled and we are on our way. We are all worried that she will not have the strength to survive our trip to America. No one has said anything, but we are all wondering if we will have to put off this trip to until Grandmother is strong enough to travel.

Father sees two men walking behind us. They are wearing armor and carrying swords on their belts. There are spears strapped over their backs. They are about one hundred paces back and slowly gaining on us.

Father says, "Let's pick up the pace."

We round a corner and see six more men ahead of us and coming toward us. They too are carrying weapons. This is exactly what all of us feared when we set off on this road. But this is worse. Not one group of robbers, but two. Father and I look at each other and we each reach for the clubs that we brought along.

Father commands, "Women, mount the horses and be prepared to ride away."

The Baroness hands her reins to Mother, picks up a club then stands shoulder to shoulder between Father and me. I think to myself, I should have expected that. I quickly glance to my side at the Baroness and am set aback to see. That lovely young lady with the magical smile has put on her war face. She has transformed into a vicious warrior, prepared to kill or die. She is focused on the enemy and planning her defense.

The six men that are coming at us from the front draw their swords and clubs. They are now just thirty feet in front of us. They stop, line up and appear to be getting ready to attack. I hear the two men that are behind us start running at us in lockstep with their footsteps sounding as one. I turn around to face them and see the two warriors each with a spear in one hand and a sword in the other. While at a dead run, they each hurl their spears at us at precisely the same moment. The spears go over our heads. I turn around to watch the spears pierce the hearts of two of our other adversaries. Both of them fall straight back and are motionless. The two warriors that had thrown the spears run past us, at the four remaining bandits. As in a choreographed movement, they each behead an opponent and stab the last two bandits in their hearts. Six men are lying dead on the trail.

It is an amazing show of extraordinary skill. The two men then turn to us. There is blood splattered on their chest and faces. I'm expecting that they will soon be wearing our blood on their armor as well. Mother cries out in what I'm expecting to hear a plea for mercy, and says, "Otto! Dietrich! My God, it's Otto and Dietrich!"

Mother, Father, Anna, and I run to them and hug and kiss them. "You're alive! You're alive! My God, you are alive! We were afraid that you had died thank God, you're alive."

Tears of happiness are in all of our eyes. We are all talking at the same time.

"Where have you been for all these years?" Father asks.

Otto replies; "It's a long story. Let us just enjoy your presence for now. Where are Grandfather and Grandmother?"

Father answers in a sober tone of voice, "Grandfather died yesterday. Grandmother is laying on the travois over there, with the horses. Go say hello."

Otto and Dietrich jog over to Grandmother to find her motionless and expressionless. Otto kneels down next to her and touches her wrist. He looks up at Dietrich, "She is dead."

A time of joy and reunion has instantly turns into tragedy. Tears of happiness still moist on our faces are now tears of sadness. Again, the Baroness is standing at a distance in awe, observing the love that my family has for each other.

Grandmother is buried alongside the road. We placed a large rock to mark her grave site.

No words are spoken as we continue our trek. We are only six hours into our trip to America, and I am physically and emotionally exhausted. I'm sure that the rest of us are too.

After an hour of silence Mother predictably, is the first to speak. "Where have you boys been for all those years? We all feared that you were both dead."

Dietrich answers, "We were defeated in Napoleon's campaign against the Russians. After that war, we were recruited by a Russian general to fight with him as mercenaries for a handsome fee. We accepted his offer and fought the Qajar Dynasty in Persia. Then, because of our experience fighting with the Russian Army. The Ottoman Empire, which was at war with Russia hired us to advise their generals in the Russian battle tactics. We had obtained wealth over the years and decided to return home. When we saw that you were not there, we tracked you down. And here we are."

Father interrupts and orders, "There is a small clearing just ahead with a stream going through it. We will camp there."

When we get to the clearing, without discussion everyone goes right to work preparing the campsite and making dinner. Otto and Dietrich take a walk around the outside perimeter to check for bandits.

It's getting dark by the time we finish dinner. The Baroness and Anna are cleaning up the dishes and cooking utensils. I check on the horses. Otto and Dietrich are taking another walk around the camp's perimeter.

When Otto and Dietrich get back, Father announces, "Mother and I will take night watch for the first four hours. The Baroness and Johann will take the second four hours. Then Otto and Dietrich will take over until morning. It's been a long and stressful day. We all are looking forward to going to sleep. Father and Mother are on watch and continue sitting at the fire."

Everyone else heads off to bed.

Mother begins with, "Your parents were wonderful people, Petrus. I am so sorry for your loss. I loved them like they were

40

my own father and mother. I remember when I was fourteen years old, and my parents tragically died from the plague. Your parents took me into their home and cared for me like one of their children. When we were married at sixteen and we continued to live with them, they accepted me unconditionally. I loved your parents for everything they did. Your mother was our midwife when I delivered our children. Johann and Anna grew up knowing your mother and father as their other parents. Johann and Anna are hurting more than they let us know."

"Thank you my dear. You know that if Mother and Father were here, they would say that you must focus on our future now. You must let us go."

"You are right." Mother replies.

Father continues, "I'm hoping that we will arrive at the seaport of Grob Klein tomorrow. We can find a place to stay, for the night then I will look for a ship that will take us to America."

> *Some of the darkest times in Mecklenburg's history were between 1820 and 1860. The peasant classes were most affected. As conditions became unbearable, 281,000 peasants left Mecklenburg, amounting to 60% of its population. The majority emigrated to America. Other countries they went to were Canada, Russia, Argentina, South Africa, Brazil, and a variety of European countries. For assorted reasons, Emigrants that came from Mecklenburg traveled with other Mecklenburgers. Of the emigrants that went to the USA most of them went to Wisconsin. The main destination was the Southeastern part of the state. Mecklenburgers that arrived later in the 19th century went to Shawano and Sheboygan counties. Other states that many Mecklenburgers emigrated to Virginia, Texas, and North Carolina.*

Now it's the Baroness and my turn for the night watch. The evening has turned cool and a damp ground fog rolled in. I add some wood to the fire to a bring it to a warming blaze. We sit down near the fire. I realize that this is the first time since we've known each other that we have been alone. I reach over, pick up a stick and I'm nervously poking at the fire.

It has been several minutes since we sat down, and we haven't spoken a word. I wonder what she's thinking about as she's staring at the fire. What an amazing moment this is. I hope that she feels the same way. I have never experienced anything like this. Until now, there has never been anyone in my life that has made me feel like this. I feel happy just being with her.

Suddenly, a feeling of insecurity and panic overcomes me. I'm thinking, "Am I the only one that is feeling this way?"

The Baroness stands, and as she's walking toward me, she asks, "Can I sit next to you?"

Without waiting for an answer, she sits down next to me, and then shuffles in closer. Now the words begin to flow. We are talking about our favorite things, and then we're talking about the things that annoy us. One subject is flowing into the next. There is so much I want to know about her and so many things that I want to tell her. The Baroness lets me know that her mother and father were subjects that she would not talk about. So, they're off limits. We talked about the fact that we have so little in common, yet we enjoy being together so much.

I don't know if I've ever been happier. She is the only thing that exists in the world for me at this moment.

Suddenly, from behind us, two men wielding swords come running. One of them jumps over the fire and runs past me to my right. The other runs past me to my left. It's Otto and Dietrich running at a group of maybe six or eight men in the shadow. The Baroness and I jump to our feet. There is a skirmish in the darkness, but I can't see what's going on. I hear swords clanking and screams of pain. I step in front of the Baroness to protect her and she pushes me aside. Then, the sound of men running. Now, two men are walking toward us into the light. It's Dietrich and Otto. Dietrich is bleeding from his left shoulder

Father and Mother are now awake, and standing with us at the fire. Otto and Dietrich are angry. They walk toward us and are standing across the fire from me. I have never seen them this angry before. As Dietrich's eyes are scanning the darkness, he speaks in a loud voice saying to me, "You were on post! You failed to do your damn job! You could have gotten us all killed! Are you a man or a lovesick child!"

Otto is right. I did fail to do my job. I failed my family. I had one thing to do and it was to keep watch. I was to watch out for the most important people in my life. Speaking in a meek manner I say, "You are right, I failed you. I failed you all. I am so sorry. I promise you all, that it will never happen again."

The Baroness speaks, "I too am responsible. It was my job as well. I allowed myself to be distracted. I apologize to you all."

Everyone is quietly watching her speak we know how difficult it must be for her to humble herself to peasants.

After a moment's pause, Father orders, "We have one hour until sunrise, let's break camp. Don't forget to wake up Anna."

Chapter Three
HMS Hopewell

Today thankfully, has been uneventful. It's mid-afternoon. We have arrived at the harbor, and it smells like an outhouse on a Sunday morning. The ships that are moored alongside the jetty are huge. I never could have imagined that the ships would be this large. Cargo is being unloaded. This is the busiest place I have ever seen.

Father announces to us, "Listen to me, I'm going to talk to someone on these ships and arrange passage to America."

After talking to the ship captains, Father returns with a disheartened expression on his face. He motions to Mother and after talking to her for a while, addresses us, "Here is what I have learned. Ships in this harbor don't go to America. For us to go to America we must first sail to England. In England, we must board another ship that goes to America. One Captain that I talked to said that he is going to a port called Liverpool, England. Most of the shipping that goes to America departs from Liverpool. He does have room for us on his ship. It departs tomorrow morning.

Here is the bad news. It costs twenty-one thaler per person to sail to Liverpool. The Captain said that we can expect to pay 100 thalers per person for tickets to sail from Liverpool to America. I had no idea that it would cost that much! I don't have enough money for us to go to America.

Dietrich speaks up, "Otto and I are going to pay for our own fares."

"I know you are Dietrich. I don't have enough money for the rest of us to go to America." Father continues, "Johann, I'm going to buy tickets for you, Anna, and the Baroness to go to America. Your mother and I decided we will stay here in Mecklenburg, until I can save enough money to join you in America. Don't try to talk us out of staying here. This is our final decision."

There is silence. Then after what seemed to be forever, with tears welling up in her eyes, Anna cries out, "I'm not going to America without you."

Before she can finish I speak over her, "We are a family, and we aren't leaving without you! Is there a way that we can go to America at a lower price? Or is there a different place that we can go together that is less expensive?"

The Baroness is standing back and listening to my family talk about our quandary. She has never experienced such love and selflessness in her life. She reaches under her blouse and pulls out a silk pouch, that was hanging around her neck. With the pouch in hand, the Baroness steps forward and says, "Put your money away, Petrus. I will pay for all of us to go to America." She then looks at Otto and Dietrich. "You can afford to pay for your own fare, okay?"

Father quickly objects to Sophia's offer. His stubborn Mecklenburger pride won't permit him to allow a woman to pay for his family to travel to America. Mother knows how to handle Father in these kinds of situations. She begins with, "You are absolutely right Petrus. We can't allow it." She walks over to him and puts her arm under his and leads him away. I have seen it a hundred times before. Mother will talk to Father and convince him that it's in the best interest of our family. When she's finished with him, he will leave their conversation convinced that it is in the best interest of our family to allow the Baroness to pay for our fare to go to America.

When we were in the labor compound and the Baroness had to get rid of her expensive clothing, the Baroness had removed her ruby rings and gold necklaces. She also cut off the silver buttons from her dress and cape. She put them all in a pouch before trading them for peasant clothing.

The Baroness says, "I have only one condition before I buy passage for us to go to America. You must stop calling me Baroness. Please call me, Sophia. I renounced the title of baroness when I left the castle and joined all of you."

Father and Sophia walked to the ship and paid for passage to Liverpool. The captain told father that he will allow us to stay onboard tonight. He said that we can board after the longshoremen are finished loading the cargo.

The ship that will take us to Liverpool is the HMS Hopewell. It is a 400-ton, three-mast clipper ship. Her captain and owner is Thomas Boyle. In years past, Boyle was a British privateer. Privateers are simply the name for government condoned piracy. The HMS Hopewell was pirated from the Dutch in a small colony named The Republic of Suriname. Suriname is located on the northeast coast of South America.

Shortly before sundown. The first mate comes to us and lets us know that we can board the ship. So, we go on board and choose a berth.

I wake up to the sound of passengers boarding. After all the passengers are aboard and the gangplank is raised, I can feel the ship begin to move. This is so exciting! The captain told Father that if the winds are favorable, we will be docking in Liverpool, England in six days.

We are out of harbor now so the captain is allowing all of us to go up to the quarterdeck. As I get to the top of the steps, I look up to see the sails have been raised on the mainmast and foremast. I feel a jerk forward as the sails are catching the wind. We are on our way! The first mate is barking orders to the sailors that are up on the masts.

Spirits are good among the passengers. We are all leaving Mecklenburg to find a better home. We are confident that there is a better place for us over the horizon.

On the morning of the sixth day on the HMS Hopewell, I get out of bed and go up to the quarterdeck. I am surprised to see that our ship is anchored off of a huge harbor. When I ask, a sailor tells me that it's the Port of Liverpool. He says that we are anchored out here waiting for the sun to rise so that we can enter the port. As it's getting lighter, I see that there are twenty other ships anchored all around us out here.

It's taking an hour for our ship to sail into the harbor and tie up at our assigned pier. While the ship is docking, our family has gathered on deck with six other families that we will be traveling with to America. It's decided that when we debark, two of us will find a place to stay while we are in Liverpool, two men will find a ship for us to take to America, and two men will stay with the families. A man named Gilbert and I are trying to locate a ship that is going to America.

I never dreamed that there were so many countries in the world until today! We didn't find one that is going to America, but we found out that the building that I thought is a castle is actually called the Port Building. The Port Building has a list of every ship that is in port, with their destination. The building is closed now, but it will be open at seven o'clock in the morning. The list is in English, so I'll bring Sophia along with us when we go there tomorrow.

The two men that were looking for a place for us to spend the night, reported that the inns that they went to are very expensive and no one would accept Mecklenburg currency. So, they found a pier that the Port Authority is allowing travelers like us to camp for the night. It's decided that we will spend the night there.

Gilbert, Sophia, and I are in line at the Port Building when it opens this morning. We find many ships posted that are going to America. Most of the ships bound for America are docked on pier number thirty-eight through pier number forty five. The three of us hurry over to those piers. On pier forty we find a group that is speaking German, so we introduced ourselves. They say that they are from Pomerania and Mecklenburg. It is wonderful to find people from my country among all of these people from all over the world. After a few minutes of conversation, one of the Mecklenburgers tells us that they are already booked on the ship that we are standing in front of. The ship is the HMS Chandler Price.

We thank our new friends and go on board to meet with the ship's Purser. He tells us that there is room for us and that the ship leaves for America tomorrow. Gilbert tells the purser that we will talk to our people and return later today.

We hurry back to tell everyone about the ship that we found. All of the men in our group went back to the HMS Chandler

Price and booked our passage to Baltimore Maryland. Father decides that we will stay at the Inn where the Mecklenburgers that we met this morning are staying. It's about ten blocks from the harbor.

We are told that this part of Liverpool can be dangerous. Father orders, "Stay together ladies. Dietrich, Otto watches out for our women."

Walking to the inn among the two-story buildings is another new experience for me. There are so many buildings and so many people!

As we enter the inn and my eyes adjust to the dark. My first thought is that this place has a strong smell of ale. Ale and smoke. Father finds the Innkeeper and pays him. We follow him upstairs to our room. The room is small with three woven rope beds in it. There are no windows, just an oil lamp for light. I was looking forward to sleeping on a bed tonight, but it looks like I'll be sleeping on the floor. As the owner is walking away, Sophia says in a loud voice, "Wait! Where do we bathe?"

The Innkeeper replies, "There is a room with a barrel in it off the back of the barroom. The water pump is outside the back door. Bring your own soap."

Sophia was not accustomed to hearing that kind of answer. To my surprise, she holds her tongue.

Father, Dietrich and Otto go downstairs to the pub for a pint of ale. Ladies aren't allowed in pubs, so the women and I stay in our room. After the men go downstairs, Mother gives me three pence to run down stairs and bring back a jug of ale and some cups. We can hear the patrons below us in the pub singing. They are singing songs like, "Nellie Dean Underneath the Arches" and "Knees Up Mother Brown."

After a couple of pints of ale, the ladies and I are singing along with them in our room. I wake up to the sound of Father and Mother packing. Everyone else is sleeping. As I'm becoming more awake, I realize that I'm in one of the beds. I sit up on the edge of the bed and look behind me in my bed and see, Sophia! She is sound asleep, so I quickly jump up to my feet and look again to make sure that it really is her. Yep, it is! How did this happen? I was supposed to sleep on the floor. I look at the person that is sleeping on the floor, and it's Otto. He's going to be angry at me! I'm going to have to stay away from him today.

The Town Caller is walking down the street in front of the Inn. He's ringing his bell and calling out, "Five o'clock and all is well. Five o'clock and all is well."

Father orders, "Time to get up!" Again, Father orders in a loud voice, "Everyone get up! It's time to get up!"

Anna groans, "I can't get up. Leave without me. I'll meet you in America. My head hurts." Father looks down at Anna and commands, "Get up!" Anna rolls out of bed. Within ten minutes we were all walking out the door and on our way to the harbor. Father reminds Otto and Dietrich, "I was warned that this is a dangerous part of the city, keep your eyes open."

HMS Chandler Price.

Chapter Four
HMS Chandler Price

A line to board the HMS Chandler Price has already formed. We step up to take our place in line. I take Sophia's hand, look her in the eyes and say, "Sophia, it's really happening. We are on our way to our new home, America. Together we will find a place that is our very own and build our new life together."

The line is becoming jam-packed. There's some bumping and pushing. It sounds like everyone is speaking a different language. I'm still holding Sophia's hand. I don't want to lose her in this crowd. I look at Mother and Father and see that they are holding hands as well. Dietrich has his hand on Anna's shoulder and is holding her firmly. A man in uniform approaches the top of the gangplank and begins taking tickets. The line is moving now! I give Sophia's hand a little squeeze. I think to myself, "We are on our way. This is exciting!"

We hand our tickets to the officer as we board the ship and continue following the line to a door and down two flights of steps to the passenger's deck. A man in uniform is standing at the bottom of the steps. He is instructing the passengers to choose a berth. He is ordering the passengers to fill each berth with at least five people. Like the HMS Hopewell, the bunks are stacked three bunks high. There are five neatly folded wool blankets on each bunk. Father chooses two berths for our family, turns to us, and says, "This will be our home for the next two weeks." We put our belongings on the berth in the space in which we will be sleeping.

Dietrich suggests that we all go up to the main deck. We follow Dietrich upstairs and to the poop deck located back of the ship. Up here we find a place to sit down and watch the sailors prepare to cast off.

Just three weeks ago my world was only one square mile in size. I knew almost everyone in my world. Everyone spoke the same language and wore the same kind of clothing. We all did the same kind of work and ate the same kind of food. We all lived in the same kind of homes, and many of the people in my world were related to me. I knew everything about them, and they knew everything about me. My world was so simple then I didn't have any idea how big and dangerous it is out here.

Now, my world extends over continents. I don't speak the same language as most of the people in this new world that I'm in. These people around me have very little in common with me. But there is one thing that everyone on this ship does have in common though. We all have a dream. Every one of us who is on this ship is escaping hopelessness. We all understand the risks and dangers ahead of us. We know that it could cost our lives to achieve our dream. We all accept the risk..

I feel a little jerk. I look around to see that the ship is beginning to slowly move away from the dock. Sophia taps my shoulder and points up. I look up to see sailors up on the masts. they are dropping the sails that were stowed on the cross masts. As the sails drop down, they catch the wind. I can feel our ship moving a little faster now. We are moving past the ships that are moored in the harbor. Sophia tugs on my sleeve. I turn around and see a huge four mast clipper ship sailing right past us. It is heading into the harbor. Passengers from our ship and the passing ship are waving and shouting out to each other in so many languages that I can't understand. I move closer to Sophia, and I put my arm around her. She turns her head and smiles with excitement. Then she leans into me and gets up on her tippy toes then kisses me on my cheek. She sets back down on her heels, looks up into my eyes, and says, "We are on our way to America Johann." I kiss her on her forehead and then wrap my arms around her and hold her tight. As I'm holding her, I'm feeling mixed emotions about leaving everything and everyone that I've ever known for what I'm praying will be a brighter future.

The ship is now leaving the protection of Liverpool Harbor.

I look around at the people around me. Everyone is looking forward. Not one single person is looking back.

All the passengers are in good spirits. They are greeting each other in their native language with a smile. I haven't seen any disagreements since we boarded. My family has been on the main deck all afternoon enjoying the ride. There is so much to take in. We have been watching the crew putting up all the sails. It took at least three hours to complete.

The weather is pleasant. It's sunny and the temperature is just a bit cool when a cloud passes overhead.

The HMS Chandler Price is a clipper ship. It was built at the Glasgow shipyard in Glasgow, England. The letters "HMS" represent "His Majesty's Ship," indicating that it is a ship of the Royal Navy, or a ship registered for service in the Royal Navy in times of war. The name "Chandler Price" is for industrialist, Sir Chandler Price who owns the ship. It's the premier ship in his fleet, so he put his name on it.

The word "clipper" is derived from the English term "clip" which means to move swiftly and is assigned to any fast-moving ship. Clippers are basically merchant vessels designed for speed. Clipper ships were first used by the British after the war of 1812. There are several types of clippers. The HMS Chandler Price is a hybrid called an "extreme clipper." Typical sailing ships before the clipper could travel 150 miles per day. A conventional clipper can travel 250 miles per day. The Chandler Price can go as fast as 20 nautical miles per hour or 400 miles per day. *

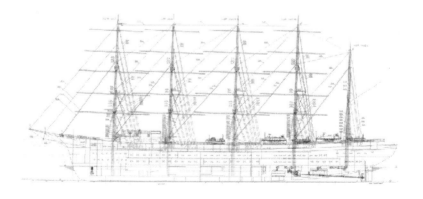

The ship's bell rings five times, indicating that it is five o'clock. The cook's assistant announces supper ringing a triangle. We all go down to the steerage deck, grab a tin plate and get in line. While in line I'm told that tonight we will be dining on a boiled potato and a biscuit. I'm hungry and I'm looking forward to breakfast. The table is twelve feet long with bench seats. The other people at our table don't speak German, Sophia is the only one in our family who is able to have a conversation at the table. The rest of us are just exchanging pleasant smiles and nods to the people across the table.

As we are finishing dinner, Anna says, "It will be nice having someone else besides me rinsing off the plates and after dinner."

After we eat, Sophia and I go up to the main deck and the rest of our family stays on the steerage deck. There are some people speaking German, so Sophia walks over to them and asks, "Sprachen sie Deutsch?"

One of the men replies, "Ja, dastun wir. Woher kommst du?" (Yes we do speak German? Where are you from?)

Sophia, "Mecklenburg. Und ja, dastun wir woher kommst du?" Sophia sits down and begins talking with them. Sophia has conversed with no one but my family since we escaped the castle. When she lived in the castle, she rarely was allowed to talk to anyone from outside the world. Now it's my turn to stand at a distance and watch Sophia. I can see that she is yearning to meet new people and learn about them. Where they lived and what it is like where they came from. I'm enjoying standing back and watching Sophia. Her eyes are wide open and focused on every word they say. She is asking questions and listening carefully to the answers. Sophia has escaped the constraints of her father's bondage. It has made a new person of her, and she is loving it.

I wake up to the ship's bell ringing six times. Our first night on board the ship went well. Dietrich, Otto, and Father are awake and on the main deck. I think I'll go up there and join them.

Today is a bit windier than yesterday. The waves still appear to be about four feet. There are a lot of people on the main deck. People are grouping with others that speak the same language as they do. Dietrich is talking to a man, so Otto and I introduce ourselves and join the conversation. "Meet Alex Becke," Dietrich says.

"Alex and his wife are from Mecklenburg. Alex is talking to me about a place called Wisconsin. He says it is a primitive place with massive forests that are beginning to be cut down by logging companies. Alex said that jobs are plentiful at good wages for men that want to work for the lumber companies. He is telling us that after the land has been logged, the lumber barons are selling the land at cheap prices to men that want to farm it."

That gets my attention, it's my dream to farm my own land. I ask, "Please, tell me more about Wisconsin. Do you know where it is? How do I get to Wisconsin? Are you going there? Is there a road that goes to this Wisconsin you speak of?"

Alex answers, "Let me introduce you to my friend, he can answer your questions." Alex calls out, "Fritz come over here please."

A short balding man walks over to us. "Fritz, meet Johann. Johann is interested in Wisconsin."

Fritz says, "It's nice to meet you, Johann. My name is Fritz Schultz. The group that I am traveling with are going to Wisconsin Territory. I work for the Kilbourn Development Company, located in Kilbourn Town, Wisconsin. I am guiding these people to their new homes in Kilbourn Town. My boss is Byron Kilbourn, and my job is to promote his new town.

Kilbourn directed me to tell everyone I meet that he is building a beautiful new town in the southeastern part of Wisconsin Territory. Johann, I'm a sales agent for Kilbourn development and I'm paid for everyone that I bring to Kilbourn Town and sell a house to them. That being known, I will tell you that, I have been to Wisconsin Territory, so I know what I'm talking about. Wisconsin is a vast frontier with endless forests. The trees are as tall as ninety feet high. The forests are full of wild game. Fish of all kinds are plentiful in the rivers and lakes. Ducks, geese, and other birds fill the sky. It is like nothing you have ever seen in Mecklenburg."

Otto clears his throat and speaks, "Fritz, I'm going to let you and Johann continue this conversation. Johann is the farmer in our family. He will have more interest in hearing about Kilbourn Town and Wisconsin than Dietrich and I do. So, if you excuse us, we will go below deck. It was nice to meet you, Fritz. I'm sure that I will see you again soon." Otto and Dietrich turn and walk away.

I ask, "Fritz, If I could have a few more minutes of your time, I would like to hear more about Wisconsin Territory?"

Fritz replies, "We have some time before breakfast. Would you like to sit down over there against the gunnel?"

As we are sitting down on the deck, I ask, "Is Wisconsin near Baltimore?"

Fritz smiles and says, "No my friend. It takes almost two weeks to travel from Baltimore to Kilbourn Town. Before I begin telling you about the way to get to Wisconsin, let me tell you some more about Wisconsin Territory. You must understand that Wisconsin is a fledgling territory on the far western edge of civilization. You may ask, why would my wife and I want to live in an uncivilized land like that? You need to know that native Indians are at war with the whites in Wisconsin and you may encounter Indians on the trail to get there. In addition to the Indian threat, you will have to protect yourself against bandits and wild animals on the trail to Wisconsin. Prepare yourself to climb mountains and cross dangerous rivers, on the trail."

As I'm listening to Fritz talk, I'm beginning to have second thoughts about going to Wisconsin Territory.

Fritz continues, "I know what you are thinking right now Johann. You're wondering if the risks are worth all of the rewards offered in the frontier. I understand that, so that is why I'm taking the time to lay everything out for you before I go any farther in our conversation. I won't hold anything against any man that tells me that he is not up to going into the frontier. I do not want anyone traveling with me that is going to give up along the way. Are you married? If you are, you'll need to explain all of this to your wife. And, after you tell her everything, I have told you. You must decide. Does she have what it takes to endure all the hardships."

As Fritz is saying this, I'm thinking about Sophia. Can she handle these hardships that Fritz speaks of? I think she could. Yes, I think she could, but do I want to put her through such danger and hardships? There is so much to consider. Then I'm thinking, what about Anna and Mother?

I don't want them to be in harm's way. I would never forgive myself if anything happened to them. Maybe it would be better for the women if we stay in Baltimore? I must think of the women's safety first. Maybe I should put my dreams on hold. Father can make all these hard decisions. I'll ask Father what we should do.

"Johann, are you listening to me?" Fritz asks.

The triangle is ringing indicating that breakfast is being served. Fritz says, "I've given you a lot to think about Johann. If you want to talk some more about Wisconsin Territory, I'll be available after breakfast. Let's go eat."

Sophia and Anna are already in line for breakfast when I get downstairs, so I get in line behind them. I'm looking at these girls standing in front of me, and I think to myself. These two girls along with Mother are the most precious people in my life. Why in the world would I consider putting them in danger? Maybe I should just find a job in Baltimore. I can put off my dream of owning my own farm for a while and get a job as a carpenter. My train of thought is interrupted when the cook's assistant says, "Here is your potato sir, hold your pan up please." Sophia leads us to the table, and we sit down for breakfast.

I want to tell Sophia about my conversation with Fritz, but I think that I had better talk to Father first. So, after breakfast, I excuse myself and hunt down Father. He and Mother are up on the main deck talking to some of their new friends, so I join in their conversation. When the opportunity arises, I pull Father aside and ask him if he can talk with him for a little while. We walk toward the stern of the ship. As we are walking, I'm telling him about my conversation with Fritz.

Then I told him that Fritz told me that he will be available to complete our conversation this afternoon. "Father, would you have interested in talking with Fritz?"

Like I thought he would, Father does want to, so we start walking around the ship looking for him. When we find Fritz, he is talking with a few men that he is traveling with. I introduce Fritz to my father and we find a place where we can sit down and talk.

I start the conversation with, "Fritz, I told my father what you and I had talked about this morning. Please tell him about Wisconsin."

I'm quiet while Fritz talks to Father about the things that we had talked about before breakfast. After informing Father of the risks and dangers of traveling to the frontier.

Fritz says, "You might ask, why would I want to go to Wisconsin? If you asked that question to the people that I'm traveling with, you would hear a variety of answers. One man may say, that he is going so that he can find affordable land to have a farm of his own. Another man might answer, by saying that he wants to escape government control and taxes. Others are going there to get away from the wars among European Kings. Some want to be able to open a business or, just be able to get a good paying job and own an affordable home for his family that he can call his own. Every one of them has a dream and they are betting that Wisconsin is where they will find it!"

Father is quiet. He's looking at Fritz. I'm thinking, "say something Father. What are you thinking?"

Fritz asks Father, "Well, what are you thinking Mr. Kemp?"

Father answers, "Must I buy a house from Kilbourn Development Company if my family travels to Wisconsin with you? Because I would not buy anything from you without seeing the town and making sure that it is where my family and I want to live."

Fritz replies, "I'm not telling you that you must buy a house in Kilbourn Town from me. There are many other options as to where you can live in Wisconsin. Fritz glances to his left and right as if looking to see if there is anyone in hearing distance. He leans forward and says, this is for your ears only, I know Byron Kilbourn. I don't trust him, and I wouldn't buy anything from Kilbourn myself."

Father pauses for a moment and then busts out laughing. Then Fritz and I look at each other and we begin laughing. As I'm laughing, I'm looking at Fritz and thinking that I really like this guy.

After he catches his breath from laughing, Father asks, "Fritz, you said that you have been to the country of Wisconsin, tell me about it. Are there large farms like Mecklenburg? Are there large cities like Liverpool? What language do the people speak? Is there a king?"

Fritz smiles and replies, "Where do I start? Wisconsin is not a country. It is a territory of the United States of America. There are twenty-four states in America plus about five or six territories on the western edge of our country. Wisconsin is one of the territories. America is a vast country of which, I have seen only a very small part of it. I have seen very large farms in the state of Virginia. I believe they call them plantations. But most of the farms are small and are about five to twenty acres in size. Unlike Mecklenburg every farm large or small are owned by men like you and I. There are no kings or noblemen that own all the land. You asked if there are cities like Liverpool. America is comprised mainly of small towns. The larger cities that I have seen like Baltimore and Pittsburgh are far smaller than Liverpool and don't have the large buildings like the ones that you saw in Liverpool. I hope that I answered your questions. Oh, there is one other thing that you didn't ask. In America you will get to choose your own leaders. Each man will have the opportunity to place one vote for every level of government leadership Once again Father and I are speechless. I was hoping for more freedom and opportunity than I had in Mecklenburg. What I am hearing about America is beyond anything that I could have hoped for."

I ask Fritz, "Tell us about Wisconsin."

Fritz looks at me and says, "I can only tell you about the small part of Wisconsin Territory that I have seen. I have been to the southeastern corner of the territory. The town that Kilbourn is promoting for his development is located at a place that the Potawatomi Indians that are native to the area call, Milwaukee. The name has something to do with the three rivers that join in a massive swamp. Milwaukee is on the west shore of a huge lake that appears to be the size of an ocean. The Ojibwe Indians call it Michigan. I was told it means large lake in their Algonquin language."

French trappers and fur traders have been in the area for many years. Now a mix of Yankees, English, some French, and Irish have moved into the town of Milwaukee. They are clearing the forests and planting crops. Logging businesses are beginning to pop up in the Green Bay area and along the Mississippi River. Investors are talking about logging around Milwaukee but there is no one logging around Milwaukee yet. I think that Milwaukee is poised to begin growing. Those that are in a position to take advantage of the growth will make a lot of money.

Father interrupts and asks, "If you think that there will be so much money to be made in Milwaukee, why aren't you there?"

"That's a fair question, Petrus. I intend to stay in Milwaukee when I get there this time. I want to open a general store."

"That's encouraging. Do you think that there will be work for a couple of carpenters in Milwaukee?"

Then, before Fritz can answer, Father asks, "Tell me about how one gets to this Wisconsin you speak of."

Fritz replies, "After we arrive in Baltimore Harbor, we will take a steamboat up the Susquehanna River to a town called

Harrisburg. Out of Harrisburg, we are going to travel west by road to Wisconsin Territory. Wisconsin is on the American frontier. It will take us two weeks to get there from Baltimore. Your family is welcome to join us if you like. You can let me know if you're coming with us any time before we arrive in Baltimore so talk to your family and let me know."

Father thanks Fritz for his time and tells him that he will let him know what he decides to do in the next few days. As Father and I are walking away he says, "Let me think on this today. I will talk to our family in the morning and let everyone in my family know about what we talked about and let you know what I decide.

It's the morning of the third day. The cook's triangle rings, and I follow my father and brothers down to the steerage deck for breakfast. We are having a boiled potato and a biscuit for breakfast just like yesterday. We have two meals per day on board and I think it will be a boiled potato and a biscuit for every meal. During breakfast, Father begins talking to Mother, Sophia, and Anna about the conversation we had with Fritz yesterday morning. Father and I like everything that we heard about Wisconsin Territory. Dietrich and Otto do not. They have no interest in being a laborer for the lumber barons or a farmer. As Otto explains it, "I spent my first 18 years working in the fields and caring for farm animals. That is not what I want to do."

Dietrich agrees, "Wisconsin sounds like it is the ideal location for you and Father. Otto and I are going elsewhere."

Mother pleads with my brothers briefly to reconsider but concedes. She knows her sons will follow their own ambitions ultimately. Mother's fear is that their ambitions will be dangerous. We all have lengthy conversations about Wisconsin

Territory. Father tells the ladies about what the trip will be like. He covers all the aspects that he can think of concerning going to Wisconsin Territory. When Father is finished, the women tell us they will go along with the plan.

I talked to the captain this morning and he is anticipating that we will arrive in Baltimore in six days. I am beginning to see that the passengers are getting a little anxious. There have been a few disagreements between some of the women. It is kind of entertaining watching them argue in their native tongues. Of course, neither of them knows what the other is saying. Otto and Dietrich's military background has taught them how to cope with boredom. The routine of having nothing to do all day is difficult for many of the passengers. I thank God that I have Sophia to talk to. We can just sit and talk for hours and the time just flies by. Sophia and I are enjoying this time just being together. I look forward to the times after a meal when Sophia and I can find a place that we can sit and talk. Recently, our conversations include planning our future together. We are so compatible in so many ways. The words marriage and children have even come up occasionally.

I talked to the captain this morning and he is anticipating that we will arrive in Baltimore in six days. I am beginning to see that the passengers are getting a little anxious. There have been a few disagreements between some of the women. It is kind of entertaining watching them argue in their native tongues. Of course, neither of them knows what the other is saying. Otto and Dietrich's military background has taught them how to cope with boredom. The routine of having nothing to do all day is difficult for many of the passengers. I thank God that I have Sophia to talk to. We can just sit and talk for hours and the time just flies by. Sophia and I are enjoying this time just being together. I look forward to the times after a meal when Sophia and I can find a place where we can sit and talk. Recently, our conversations include planning our future together. We are so compatible in so many ways. The words marriage and children have even come up occasionally.

It's getting dark and the temperature is dropping, so I put my cloak over Sophia's shoulders. The watchman in the crow's nest calls out, "Storm ho! Storm approaching!"

Sailors are immediately climbing the masts and taking rigging down. Winds are quickly picking up and waves are crashing over the side of the ship. Passengers are running for cover. Sophia and I run to the stairs. The ship's bow swings sharply and the ship lists to the starboard. Someone calls out, "Man overboard! Man overboard!"

The wind and rain continue to increase. The wind is blowing so hard that we aren't able to stand up on the wet deck. We drop to our hands and knees and are crawling to the stairs. The driving rain is only allowing us to see about ten feet now. Passengers are screaming and calling for their loved ones.

We find the stairs and slide down the steps to the steerage deck. It's dark down here with only the dim light from a few port holes to light the room. The thrashing we are receiving has made us disoriented.

Sophia and I are trying to find my family. Exhausted, we sit down on a bench at one of the dining tables. After about ten minutes, I feel that the wind and rain is beginning to let up a bit. We can't stand up yet because the waves are still high, but they are down substantially from what they were.

Sophia says, "look," and points to the sun streaming through one of the portholes.

Skies are clearing and the wind has calmed to ten miles per

hour. I'm calling for my family and walking around the dark steerage deck.

Frantically, Sophia calls to me, "Come quickly, it's your father!"

I come running, slip on the wet floor and get right up. There he is, laying on a bunk, not moving. Mother and Anna are by his side crying. I call for the ship's surgeon but he is working on another injured person. Father's chest is torn open and ribs are exposed. There is much bleeding. His head is crushed as well. Dietrich and Otto have seen these types of wounds and they are treating them.

Anna is calling out with tears in her eyes, "**Father, Father Save him**! **Please save him**! **Please**!

Dietrich stands up with tears in his eyes and quietly says, "He's gone."

Otto is kneeling, and drops his head on Father's shoulder, sobbing. Mother and Anna are screaming and crying. They drop down on him. I'm standing in disbelief with tears welling in my eyes.

"This can't be... My God, don't let him die!" Sophia is afraid that I'm going to collapse, and she quickly holds on to me. Otto reaches over and gently closes Father's eyes.

It is the morning after that fateful storm. Dietrich tells me that a taut line hitch that was holding a two-hundred-pound keg of nails broke loose in the storm and the keg crashed down onto Father causing his fatal injury. In addition to Father's passing, two sailors fell from the foremast. One died instantly the other isn't expected to survive his wounds. One passenger fell overboard and is presumed drowned.

All the sailors are ordered on deck and are standing at attention.

Most of the passengers are on deck for the funeral. Father along with the sailors that died are buried at sea this morning.

Our family has been able to do very little else other than mourn Father's death since he died. I am not accepting the reality of it all. Until now, I didn't realize how often I relied on him for even the smallest things. When I had a question or need some direction, Father was always there for guidance. I never realized how important he was to me until today. I lost my best friend yesterday. Goodbye Father, I love you.

Mother is just sitting by herself, despondently staring at the place where Father died. I am so worried about her. She hasn't eaten since his death. Mother had been with no one else but Father since she was fourteen years old. Anna is with her day and night. I never knew how strong Anna is until now. She is the one that is holding us all together through our sorrow and lament. The captain has announced that we will be arriving in Baltimore sometime tomorrow. It will be helpful for us to get off of this damned ship and have something to keep us busy. We all went to bed early last night, in an effort to have the morning come faster. I'm lying in bed wide awake. For the first time in weeks, I'm looking forward to the new day. I'm lying in our berth staring at the cot above me. I hear the ship's bell ring five times. Today is the last day of what seems to be an ocean voyage that would never end.

Dietrich and Otto are both up already and outside on the main deck. I get out of bed to go topside. Sophia and Anna follow me. We join my brothers standing at the front of the ship.

"Good morning, Otto. Good morning, Dietrich."

Otto replies, "I will be glad to get the hell off of this damned ship today!"

We all smile. It's the first time any of us had smiled in days. I think we are all feeling blessed to be together. Anna acknowledges that Sophia is part of our family by walking over to her and giving her a hug. Tears are forming in my iron lady's eyes. I've never seen her show any emotion before.

I need a little time to be alone, so I take a walk up to the quarterdeck. How lucky I was to have a father like he was.

A passenger I know that is bunking above me comes over to me to tell me that I should check on my mother. I hurry down to the lower deck. When I get to the bottom of the stairs, I see that the ship's surgeon is with Mother.

I hurry over to her and the surgeon says to me, "Your mother doesn't have much time left. You and your family should say goodbye to her. I think to myself, this can't be true. She can't be dying. I can't lose her too!" Mother is lying motionless with her eyes closed. She is so peaceful, barely breathing. I fall to my knees and hold her hand. It is cold. Tiers are running down my face. She seems to be sleeping.

The surgeon steps forward and touches her wrist for a short while then sets it down and says to me, "I'm sorry, she has passed." Sophia comes down to check on me. She sees me kneeling next to my mother weeping and quietly comes to me and kneels next to me. She puts her hand around my shoulder and holds me. After hearing about my mother's passing, the captain comes to me and my brothers to convey his condolences. He tells us that we will be in Baltimore harbor this afternoon. He said that when we arrive in port, he will contact an undertaker to make arrangements for Mother's burial.

He goes on to say, "If you like I will arrange for your parents' funeral on board after we dock."

Chapter Five
On to Wisconsin

After we dock and the sails and rigging are stowed. Mother and Father's funeral is held onboard the ship. Many of the passengers, ship's officers, and crew are attending.

When the funeral is concluded, Otto asks the men to join us at a saloon that is down the street to celebrate Mother and Father's life.

Anna invited the women and children to join Sophia and herself at the park that is across the street from the saloon for ice cream.

At the saloon, we made a few toasts to Mother and Father and shared some fond memories of them. Dietrich is telling funny stories about Father that have us all laughing. Then he begins telling us about his memories of Mother and her kind heart. After a few pints of ale, most of the men leave.

For those of us that are going to Wisconsin, the conversation turns to our journey to Wisconsin Territory.

A man named Wilhelm makes a count of everyone that will be traveling with us. At this time, we will be traveling with seven families. Five families are from Mecklenburg, and two families are from Pomerania. There are nine children under the age of fifteen. We'll have four boys and two girls over fifteen years old.

The meeting continues. Fritz says, "I will find a schooner that can take us up the Chesapeake Bay to Perryville, Maryland. Perryville is at the mouth of the Susquehanna River. There are many ships traveling to Perryville daily so I am confident that I can find one that will take us tomorrow. We will stay in Perryville tomorrow night. In Perryville, we will board a steamboat and sail up the river to Harrisville. We will spend the night there. In Harrisville we will buy wagons and horses for our journey overland to Wisconsin. Those of you that don't require a wagon can buy a handcart. There are several shops that make hand carts in Harrisburg. You will buy your supplies for the overland trip in Harrisburg as well. I have given you all a list of items you will need. Are there any questions?"

There are none. "Okay then. You will make your own arrangements for your lodging tonight. There are several hotels nearby. We will meet here tomorrow morning at seven o'clock."

In 1829, Baltimore Harbor is the third largest seaport in America ranking behind New York and Boston Harbors. Tobacco is Baltimore's main export commodity. More tobacco is shipped from Baltimore than anywhere in the world.

There are four major shipyards located in Baltimore Harbor: Harris Creek shipyard, George Wells Shipyard Spencer's Shipyard, and Fells Point Shipyard.

Fort McHenry can be seen on Locust Point. Famous for defending Baltimore against the British while being bombarded during the war of 1812 *

* Wikipedia

After our meeting, my brothers and I walk to the park to meet Sophia and Anna. We check into a nearby hotel. There, we tell the women about our meeting. The five of us talk about what we need to prepare for the trip to Wisconsin Territory. After our little meeting with the ladies my brothers and I walk to a saloon that is located down the street and continue planning our trip.

Some of the patrons at the bar we are speaking in German and talking about an Indian war that broke out in Alabama. Otto and Dietrich are listening intently.

Otto asks, "What is Alabama? Where is this Alabama?"

One of the bar patrons' answers, "It is a new state located down South."

With further inquiry Otto learns that, President, Andrew Jackson is recruiting men to join the fight against the Muskogee Indian Nation.

> *The Muskogee tribe is also known as the Creek tribe. In 1828 the Creeks number 20,000. They are in Alabama, Georgia and north Florida. After Alabama became a state, Congress ordered the Creeks to turn their lands over to the US government. President Andrew Jackson ordered General Winfield Scott to round up all of the Creeks and move them to Indian Territory. (Oklahoma) The Creek Nation chief, Opothle Yohola, resisted resulting in the bloody Creek war. ***

Dietrich and Otto agree that this may be the opportunity that they have been looking for.

* Wikipedia

After learning about the Creek War yesterday, Dietrich and Otto talk about their options and decide to enlist in the US Army to fight in the Creek War. They're saying that it's the patriotic thing to do for their new country. I know better. They miss the excitement of war. They found out that the Army recruiting station is in Washington DC.

"We should leave for Washington tomorrow. Let's let Anna and Johann know our plans." says Dietrich.

Anna, Sophia and I walked to the stagecoach station with our brothers at two o'clock. When the stage arrives, we hug them good-by. Otto and Dietrich climb into the coach and they are on their way.

As I'm waving goodbye I'm praying. "God protect them."

After the Stagecoach is out of sight, Sophia, Anna, and I leave the stagecoach station. I'm feeling sad that my brothers are gone, and I can see that Anna is too.

Sophia says, "Let's find a hotel that we can stay at tonight. We should find one near the port because we will need to meet our group early in the morning." I nod in agreement.

As we are walking toward the harbor, I realize that I am the man of the family now. Father is gone, Grandfather died, and now Dietrich and Otto just left. I'll need to make all of the decisions for now on. I look at Anna and Sophia as they're talking to each other, and say to myself, "They're under my care now. I just hope that I am able to do the job as well as they did."

We find a hotel and check into it. There is a saloon below our room that is patronized by sailors and longshoremen. I've never heard anything like it before. There was a piano playing, loud talking and fights. The noise kept us awake until the bar closed at 3:00!

We are up and out of the hotel and meet our traveling companions. Fritz leads us all to the ship. It's a two-mast schooner that is much smaller than the ships that we had traveled on before.

The day is passing quickly. I'm able to see the shore on the starboard side of the ship the entire day. At around four o'clock, the first mate starts barking orders. The sailors begin hurrying around the ship. Some of them are climbing the masts and lowering some of the sails. I walk to the front of the ship, and I can see the mouth of a river. As we are getting closer, I can see that there is a town on the right bank with ships docked in a harbor. I think to myself, "that must be Perryville."

We debark in Perryville and check into a hotel. I buy a jug of beer at the hotel bar then Anna, Sophia and I go out on the front balcony and sit down on some benches. Sophia and Anna are becoming very good friends. The two of them are talking and laughing. In fact, they are having so much fun talking to each other that they aren't including me in their conversation. I think I'll just take the jug of beer and go to our room. I'll bet that they won't even notice that I'm gone. I get up from the bench and reach for the jug.

Sophia turns to me and says, "Are you going to bed? Leave the beer." She then turns back to Anna and continues talking.

It's morning and we are on the paddle boat named Sally Ann and, on our way, up the Susquehanna River. I'm amazed that this boat is moving under power of something called an engine. The world has turned the corner to the age of mechanization. Machines can now do the work that in the past, could only be performed with muscle applied by either man or beast. I'm in awe that this machine is powering the boat against the current without anyone doing anything but putting logs in the firebox. Anna is up on the ship's command deck with all her attention directed to the ship's Captain. Anna never has shown any interest in any boy or man before. This is highly unusual. It seems that the captain is enjoying Anna's company as well. I had better check this guy out. So, I introduce myself to the Captain as Anna's older brother. Anna knows what I'm up to, so she gives me a dirty look and steps behind the captain where she motions me away.

I say, "Captain, was nice to meet you sir," and then I walk away. He seems to be a pleasant enough fellow.

He is handsome and appears to be wealthy. I think to myself, nobody is good enough for my little sister. I'll keep an eye on those two.

The trip to Harrisburg will take three days. There are bunk beds that can be rented for four cents per person per night. I rented spaces for the three of us for the two nights that we will be on board. The bunks hold four people so there will be a fourth person sleeping with us tonight. Sharing beds with strangers to reduce lodging cost is common practice on ships. The sun is going down and the crew is lighting the whale oil lamps. I haven't seen much of Anna today. She has spent the entire day with Captain McCarthy. I don't approve of this! Anna is just sixteen and McCarthy appears to be thirty years old. Sophia puts me at ease by telling me to go to the bar and have a pint of ale, and that she will go and find Anna. Well, I had a few pints and stayed at the bar until quite late in the evening.

I wake up and the sun is high in the sky. Oh no, I slept through breakfast! Most everyone is out of bed and out on the sunny side of the deck. I go up on the deck and find Sophia. She is visiting with friends. "Good morning. How did you sleep last night?" Sophia asks with an understanding smile. Most other women would come down hard on their partner for staying out late. I've only known Sophia for a short time, but she understands me. Since we met, she watched me walk away from my home and friends in Mecklenburg. Then I lost my parents and grandparents. My brothers went off to war and I may never see them again. Now my sister, who is my best friend is falling in love with someone that I fear will take her away from me.

Sophia is so smart. She gave me a quarter and sent me to the barroom last night so that she could meet Captain McCarthy and then talk to Anna without me around. She knows that she can be objective when I am not able to be. Anna and Sophia talked for hours last night. Sophia just listened while Anna talked. Anna needs a friend that she can talk to about her new love.

It's obvious that Anna is so happy and so in love. Anna is new to love, so trusting and so vulnerable. As Sophia listens, she is hoping that Anna doesn't get hurt. Sophia is thinking that just a few short weeks ago I was falling in love. Unlike Anna and there was no one that I could talk to about it.

It's the evening of the second day on board and I haven't seen Anna all day. I know that she has been with McCarthy. I've come to the realization that there is nothing I can do. I'll try to be happy for her. Sophia gives me another quarter and tells me to go to the barroom and have a pint of beer. That sounds like a good idea so I'm on my way. Until now, I have never been able to go to a bar because my father and brothers said that I was too young. I have this newfound freedom and I'm enjoying it.

It's another morning and just like yesterday I wake up and the sun is high in the sky. I missed breakfast again. Most of the other passengers are on the sunny side of the deck. And like yesterday I find Sophia talking to friends. Anna is with McCarthy again as well, I'm sure.

The boat whistle is sounding to announce our approach to Harrisburg. Sophia and I join many of the passengers hurrying to the front of the boat to see the city. Most of the people on the boat will be traveling West from Harrisburg to find opportunities and a new home in the frontier territories. The pilot steers the boat gently to the pier. The boat's crew of twenty men each has a task in mooring the boat and is hurrying to accomplish it. After the boat is hitched to the pier and the gangplank is lowered, Sophia and I go below deck to gather our belongings.

As I'm collecting my things, I realize that I haven't seen Anna this morning, but I see that her things are already packed and gone.

"Sophia, do you know where Anna is?" I ask.

"Anna is not coming with us Johann. She is going to stay on the ship with Captain McCarthy. Anna asked me to tell you because she knew that you would be angry with her. Anna told me that she is in love with the captain, and she believes that he loves her too. Anna asked me to let you know that her decision is final and you won't talk her into changing it. That is why she is avoiding you today. Anna asked me to tell you that she loves you and that you will always be her best friend."

I'm mad and hurt "Where is she? Where is McCarthy? If you don't tell me, I'll find them! He can't take my sister! I'll kill that guy!"

Sophia replies in a sympathetic tone, "They went on shore. I told them to. Johann, Anna is in love. When someone finds the person that they want to spend the rest of their life with they know it. Look at us Johann. You must let her go. She told me that she understands that she could be hurt, and she is willing to take the risk for her chance at happiness. You must let her go Johann."

I'm processing everything for a minute. Sophia is right. Anna needs to find out if this is the person that she has been looking for all her life. I've protected my little sister all of our lives. But I can't protect her anymore. It hurts me to think that I may never see her again.

The Mecklenburgers that we have been traveling with meet briefly after we debark the boat. Fritz suggests, that because no one knows how long it will take to acquire the things that we need for the journey to Wisconsin Territory we will meet here at the end of the day tomorrow.

The first thing Sophia and I will do is find a hotel for us to stay at tonight. Then, because we really don't have enough possessions to require a wagon. We decided to buy a hand cart to carry our belongings. We bought flour, potatoes and beets. I also bought a .525 caliber musket, powder, a powder horn, and four dozen musket balls.

After we buy everything that we think that we will need for the trip to Wisconsin, Sophia suggests, "Let's go to the harbor and say goodbye to Anna." When we get to the dock, the paddle boat had left. Sophia sees my sinking expression and quickly says, "Hay Johann, as soon as we arrive in Wisconsin, I will write a letter to Anna for you. We will mail it to the captain's shipping company in care of Anna."

I respond, "Maybe someday, Sophia, you can teach me how to read and write so that I can write my own letters.

We stayed at the Hotel Central last night, and we are up and out sightseeing early today. Sophia is so much fun to be with! Harrisburg is a scenic, pastoral town, compact and surrounded by farmland. It is playing a notable role in the history of America's westward expansion. The Pennsylvania Canal is under construction and someday will carry freight and passengers between Harrisburg and Pittsburgh. Completion is slated for the end of this year. For now, we will have to walk to Pittsburgh.

Harrisburg seems to be a natural debarking location for those of us that are traveling west on the Susquehanna River. In Harrisburg, we will buy the necessary items and prepare for our overland journey to the Wisconsin Territory. Some of the people on the riverboat were saying that the United States Congress authorized the construction of a military road named "The Great Lakes Military Road."

The road runs between Harrisburg, Pennsylvania, and Fort Dearborn in Illinois. We were warned that the road is nothing but a wide path that the Army Corp of Engineers cut through the wilderness. It is barely wide enough for a wagon to fit through. I was told that there are no bridges over the rivers and streams. Some of the Rivers on this side of Pittsburgh will have ferry boats for crossing rivers. We will have to forage the rivers that are beyond Pittsburgh.

> *Over time, The Great Lakes Military Road was used more and more by pioneers going west to the southern Great Lakes region. In 1870, (40 years after Johann and Sophia traveled the trail) the government added improvements to the road and named it "The Lincoln Highway." In the 1930's it was paved under Franklin Roosevelt's, "Federal Aid Highway Program" and was named "State Highway 30". Finally, under the Interstate Highway Act of 1956 and Eisenhower's National System of Interstate and Defense Highway System" it was reconstructed into four lanes and named Interstate Highway 80. ***

South of the capital are rows of single-story houses that are owned by State senators and representatives. The streets are dirt but orderly and lined with elm trees. There are no factories present. However, there are numerous stores and all kinds of trade shops, such as blacksmith and carpenter shops. Wagon works shops and horse traders that are catering to travelers like us are numerous.

> *Twenty years after Johann and Sophia left. Harrisburg found its importance in America's the steel industry. Beginning in 1850 manufacturing of steel and related businesses like steel rolling mills and steel foundries will spring up. Steel manufacturing will attract railroad and barge companies to transport steel products. Good paying jobs in the steel industry will make Harrisburg a boom town.*

* Wikipedia

81

I met with the group that is traveling with us and everyone is ready and anxious to leave for Wisconsin. It is agreed by all of us that we leave for Wisconsin tomorrow morning. This evening Sophia and I are sitting next to each other on the balcony outside our hotel room. We are watching the lamplighter as he is lighting the streetlights and, we are reflecting on our day.

Sophia turns to me and with her flirtatious giggle, punches me in the arm and says, "I haven't had time to do that in a long time. Did you miss it?"

She nuzzles close to me and puts her hand on mine. "Since the moment we met, we have never had an opportunity to spend time together like this. Just you and I, all alone. It's wonderful. I want to spend the rest of my life with you Johann."

Chapter Six

Great Lakes Trail

When I awake, the sun is just emerging over the treetops. Sophia is up and packing the last of our belongings. As I'm rolling out of bed, Sophia is taking the blanket that I slept under and begins folding it and packing it for our journey.

Our handcart was in the hotel's stable overnight. I go over to the stable and get it. I put our belongings in it, and we are on our way to meet our group.

We are all gathering at the ferry dock on the east bank of the Susquehanna River. The ferry is slowly crossing the river toward us. When it arrives at our dock, the two crewmen jump off the ferry with ropes in hand and tie it up to the dock. They quickly shuffle us onto the ferry and we are on our way to the west side of the river. It's taking about fifteen minutes to cross the river.

Some of the horses are a little spooky but a gentle rub on their noses and a calming voice puts them at ease. When the ferry arrives at the west shore. We unload and we are on our way, traveling the Great Lakes Trail!

I'm intrigued by the farms that we're passing. They appear to be between five and twenty acres each. I'm told that every farm that we are passing is owned and worked by individual landowners.

I'm thinking, "It's something that I had never seen in Mecklenburg. Everyone I pass is living my dream! I'm enlivened by the thought that someday, Sophia and I will have our own land! Our own farm! Our own house! We will harvest our own crops and raise our own poultry and livestock!"

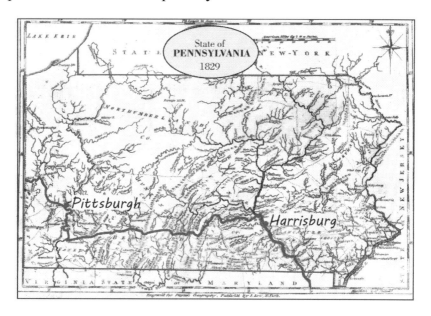

By mid-afternoon, I am noticing a slight upward grade. Fritz tells me that we are approaching the east edge of the Allegheny Mountains foothills. I can see mountain tops at a distance. I've never seen a mountain before.

Ten hours of walking today and we come to a little hamlet called Landisburg. It's really nothing but a Post Office with a whiskey still behind it. With the Postmaster's permission, we set up camp for the night near the still.

On our second day all the adults are awake and breaking camp at first light. Everyone is eager to get started this morning. Soon, the trail turns to a southwest direction following a wide valley. I see that the farms are smaller now. There are fewer of them in this valley than we saw yesterday.

I can feel that we are rising in altitude and the air is getting a little thinner. The trail is getting rougher as we continue up the mountain. Where I came from the land was flat lowland with lakes and marshes. There was nothing more than a few low hills. Here there are mountains all around us!

Deer, elk, and turkey are abundant. Heinrich, who is in our group asks me if I want to shoot some game for camp meat with him. I have not shot my new musket yet. In fact, I had never shot any musket! In Mecklenburg firearms were only available to the military for battle and nobility for hunting. I load the gun as the shop owner showed me and then put the gun in my cart until the opportunity or necessity to shoot something arises.

All of the men in our group purchased a musket for this trip. None of us had ever shot a gun before, so we all decided to stop and shoot some rounds. My gun is a model M1819 breach loading musket. It cost fifteen dollars and seventy-five cents.

The Model M1819 Hall Rifle was historically significant whereas it was the first mass- produced breech-loading rifle with interchangeable parts.

Designed by: John Hancock Hall Produced by: Harpers Ferry Arsenal, in Virginia Years produced: 1820s - 1840s

*Used in: the Mexican-American war and numerous Indian wars. Cartridge: .525 ball   Length: 52.5"   Weight: 10.25 LB Effective range: 800 - 1500 yards ***

* Wikipedia

We are all anxious to shoot our new guns, so we stop and try them. My first shot is a misfire because I loaded it wrong. After rethinking the process, I load the gun properly. After working through the procedure, we were able to have our guns shoot consistently. One of our men stuck a sheet of newspaper on a tree as a target. We all take turns shooting. No one can hit it! This is terrible. We were all assuming that these guns are going to kill game for our food and protect us from our enemies!

We must acquire the skill to shoot these muskets accurately before we go further into the wilderness. We decide to keep shooting until we can hit what we are shooting at. By the end of the day, most of us are becoming quite accurate with our new muskets. After we are finished shooting, the women have the fires burning, dinner prepared, and our tents set up for the evening.

After dinner our new friends Hans and Anita, invite us to sit around their fire and visit with them. They're telling us about where they came from and about their family. They have three young children that are, without a doubt, the most important things in their lives. Their youngest knows we are talking about her, and she comes over to me and climbs on my lap. She has curly red hair and freckles. "Little girl is your name Freckles?" I ask.

"No! My name is Olga"

"How old are you, Olga?" She holds up three fingers.

Anita's four-year-old now comes to me and stands next to my knee.

"What is your name little boy?"

"I'm Rudy, and I'm four years old. What is your name?"

Before I can respond, Anita says; "Rudy, Olga, Heidi it's time to go to bed now."

Olga turns to face me and gives me a hug around my neck and says to me, "Ni, ni."

I hug her back, "Good night sweetheart"

Sophia says, "Johann, It's your bedtime too. Say good night."

On our third day, we wake up to raindrops on the tent. It's raining hard and steady, and it doesn't look to be letting up soon. Well, let's get up and see how many miles we can put behind us today. Sophia and I put a biscuit in our mouths, bundle up the tent and place it in it the cart. We take our place in line and we are on our way.

The rain has been coming down steadily all morning. The trail is muddy and slippery. In many places, the rain is creating a small stream that's running down the trail. I see fresh bear tracks in the mud. It looks like an adult with two young cubs. The tracks indicate that they're walking up the trail ahead of us. The tracks were made since the rain started this morning. My Grandmother used to tell me fairy tales that had bears in them. Bears have always been some mystical creatures to me. But these bears are real and I know that they can kill a person.

It's late in the afternoon. It has rained continually all day. I feel soaked to the bone. Sophia is of course, as wet as I am. She hasn't complained at all. Someone up front calls out, "Does anyone want to stop and set up camp for the evening?"

We all respond with a resounding, "Ja lass uns aufhoren!"

It's the morning of day four on the Great Lakes Trail. It's a warm and sunny morning with light winds. By now everyone knows their morning chores and we are all busy doing it. I pause for a moment to watch Sophia as she is packing. She is such a hard worker and so beautiful to me. Why am I so blessed?

The altitude is affecting all of us including the horses now. It's a constant climb through Stoney Creek Pass. Fritz tells me that the snowcapped mountains that I see to the south of us is the highest point in Pennsylvania.

I'm struggling with this damned cart today. Our pace has slowed considerably, and we are stopping to rest on a regular basis now. It is getting cooler as we rise in altitude and some of us are putting on an additional layer of clothing. I am seeing items such as a plow, a cast iron bed frame, and a headboard on the side of the trail. Apparently, previous travelers had cast off items to reduce weight.

We are now seeing animals such as big horn sheep and mountain goats on the mountain sides. I never knew such animals existed.

We have reached the high point of this mountain ridge and the view is spectacular! It makes the last four hours of muscling this cart up the mountain worthwhile. The Allegheny Mountain range appears to be a series of parallel mountain ridges like ripples on a pond. We have conquered the first ripple! Well, let's get moving. Good news, walking downhill is much easier.

The trail follows an ephemeral riverbed down the mountain. The river is only a very small stream now. It took four hours to get down the mountain and now the grade is leveling off. There are signs that other travelers chose this sight to camp. It's getting late so we will stay here for the night. Everyone knows what to do to set up camp, so we all get busy doing our chores and making our evening meals.

After dinner the men gather around one of the campfires. Our discussion begins with laudatory comments amongst ourselves for conquering our first mountain ridge. The problem is that, being at the top of the mountain allows us to see the other mountains that are ahead of us. Someone points out, "At least there is one mountain ridge behind us."

One of the serious problems we must address is that food is running low for most of us. It's decided that we will pair up tomorrow and hunt for game. Two men will stay at the camp to guard it. The women and children will look for berries near our camp campsite pack of wolves are howling nearby. It's a reminder that we are not alone out here. It's beginning to lightly rain so we adjourn the meeting, and we go back to our families.

It was a physically trying day today for both Sophia and me. Tomorrow will be the same. We climb into our bed roll and are asleep before our heads hit the pillows.

I'm awakened in the night by a loud crack of thunder. It sounds close. Large beads of rain is hitting the tent roof at a slow pace. They remind me of the drummer boy tapping a slow marching gait as my brothers went to war. It is a relaxing sound, tap. . .tap. . .tap. . . Now the pace is picking up a bit, tap..tap.tap..tap. I'm falling back to sleep when a lightning bolt hits nearby and instantly a loud clap of thunder sounds.

Suddenly, the heavens open and rain is pouring down in torrents. Sophia asks, "What should we do? Are we going to be okay?"

I answer, "I think so, can't think of anything that we left outside. Let's just stay in here. I can't imagine that his rain can keep up like this, too for much longer."

After about fifteen minutes of listening to the rain pouring down, Sophia asks, "Have you ever seen rain like this before? Did it rain this much on the farms? Where does all this water go?" At that moment she is interrupted by a roaring sound outside the tent. It is coming down the mountain. Confused, we listen without speaking.

I'm lying here in the dark staring at the tent ceiling. Sophia asks, "What is that? What can that be?" I can feel the mountain shaking!

There is a roaring sound that keeps building louder and louder. I open the tent door just enough to peak out. The overcast night makes it too dark to see anything. There is something outside that sounds like cattle running down the mountain. I open the tent door just enough to look outside again. Rain is pouring in on my face. I'm not able to see anything but the stampede sounds like its getting closer. Suddenly, an enormous elk jumps over our tent. behind him are at least eight others running with him. Behind them, I can see what looks to be a wall of water coming down the riverbed! It's coming right at us, sounding like the locomotives that we heard in Liverpool.

"Look out Sophia!" And then it hit us with a force stronger than anything that I have ever felt before Rushing water is on top of us instantly. The door of the tent is facing up the mountain and the water catches our tent like a windsock. We are helplessly being hurled downstream. We are deflecting off of rocks at an unimaginable speed. Sophia and I are getting thrown about inside the tent like a couple of olives in a butter churn.

The current is so powerful. I can't survive much more of this! I slam into something hard, and we come to a sudden stop. It must have broken some ribs. Air, I need air. I can feel an air pocket at the top of the tent. I put my face up into it and take a breath. Now, where is Sophia, I must find Sophia. I'm feeling around in the dark water. There she is. Her body is limp and pressed against the back of the tent. I shake her. She's not responding. I must get her out of this tent somehow! I'm disoriented.

Where is the tent opening?"

I'm feeling along the tent wall. There, there it is! I'm out of the tent. Now I can tell that we   are hung-up on a tree. A quick breath of air and I duck back into the tent feeling around in the dark to find Sophia again. There she is. I'm fighting the current with everything that is in me. I'm able to pull Sophia out of the tent. She's not moving. "My God. Is she dead?"

I'm fighting the current, trying to keep her head above the water. She's not breathing!

"Oh God, what can I do?"

The current is pressing us up against the tree with unbelievable force! I'm working as hard as I can to keep her head up. I'm fighting to hold onto Sophia with every bit of strength that I have. She isn't moving! This can't be happening. God help me. Sophia don't leave me!

I'm holding my poor Sophia and sobbing uncontrollably. I put my arms around Sophia and squeeze her in a quick pumping action. To my surprise, she coughs and projects up a tremendous amount of water. Then coughs again She continues the deep coughing over and over.

I look up and cry out loud, "Thank you God!"

"After she stops coughing, Sophia turns her head to me, and a weak smile forms on her face.

In a loving tone, I say, "You had me so scared."

She simply smiles back at me. reaching over to me, she gives me a weak punch in my arm.

We are both shivering, and our teeth are chattering out of control. Hypothermia is setting in and we must find a way to get out of this water. Sophia has not regained her strength yet, but we have to act now.

"Hold on to me Sophia. We must get to shore."

While holding on to Sophia, I push off of the tree with my legs. Here we go! The current grabs us and is swiftly carrying us downstream like a pair of leaves. We are floating down the valley. Whirlpools are spinning us at the river's will. As hard as I try, the river is not allowing me to get to shore. We're floating downstream for what seems to me to be about a half of a mile. The river is now getting wider, and the grade is getting flatter. The water is slowing down now and gratefully, the river is slowing and allowing us to swim to shore.

Exhausted, we crawl onto the riverbank and lie on our backs in the tall grass. We're looking up and catching our breath. I realize that the clouds are gone. Stars are in the sky and are fading as the sky is getting light. We must have lain here panting for at least fifteen minutes as we regain our strength.

The sky is completely clear now. There are just a few clouds on the horizon that are indicating the trailing end of the storm. There are voices. We sit up and we can see some people walking along the riverbank in our direction. They are about two hundred yards upstream, on our side of the river. One of them looks like Fritz. He is with two people, but I'm not able to tell who the others are. Sophia and I stand up and start walking upstream along the riverbank toward them. As we are getting closer to them, we can see that the other two are Hans and Anita. Sophia turns her head and looks at me. "Johann, I don't see the children. Where are Anita and Hans' children?"

As we get closer to Hans and Anita I can hear Anita crying, uncontrollably. Hans appears to be in a state of shock.

When we approach each other, Fritz says "The children are missing," in a somber tone of voice.

"We will help you find them," Sophia says in a positive manner. She then gives Anita and Hans a sympathetic smile.

While we are talking, I'm facing upstream and can see that over Fritz's shoulder, there are five people walking in our direction. They are on the other side of the river and are at a far distance away. I point them out to Fritz and Sophia. and say in a low tone of voice. "They're searching the other side of the river."

Sophia and I begin walking downstream with Hans and Anita.

As I am walking, I'd like to tell Anita and Hans, not to worry and that everything will be alright. I'm afraid that won't be the case.

Sophia is walking next to Anita in a show of support. Sophia slows down and falls back next to me and quietly says to me, don't talk. There are no words that can be said that will make this easier for Hans and Anita. How does she know what I'm thinking?

The five of us are walking at a slow and cautious pace. We know that we are on a recovery mission. Hans and Anita's children are just three, four, and seven years old. They probably can't even swim. I want to tell Hans that he and Anita can go back to camp, and I will bring their children to them. How could I tell them such a thing?

We did eventually find young Rudy and Heidi. They were a mile down the river. Little Olga was recovered the following day when the water level went down. Fritz and Ida also lost their five-year-old child, Inga in the flood. We buried the four children on high ground and marked their graves with wooden crosses.

We choose to stay at this campsite on the riverside for three days. The water level has receded to a small stream. We are all helping Hans, Anita, Fritz, and Ida with their belongings. I'm able to find my cart downstream and remarkably, it's in working order. Our tent is still hung up on that spruce tree, so I take it down. Most of our things including our food and cooking implements are lost. My musket and musket balls are still in the tent. One of my boots is gone, but Sophia's boots are both still in the tent.

Things are looking desperate for our party. Almost all our food was washed away or is inedible. All of our musket powder was destroyed so we can't even hunt for our food. The women and children have been in the woods looking for berries while the men are retrieving and repairing wagons and carts. One of Fritz's horses has not returned. One horse alone won't be able to pull his wagon up these mountain trails. If the second horse can't be found, he will have to leave his wagon and most of his belongings behind.

What are we going to do about food? What little food that we were able to save was fed to the children. The adults haven't eaten for two days. I don't know if I have the strength to pull my cart up the next mountain! And if we are able to make it over this mountain, we have no idea what is beyond it. Will we be able to find food there? No one is saying it, but we know that our chance for survival is looking hopeless. Sophia speaks up, "I can ride Fritz's horse over the mountain and see if there is anyone over there that can help us. I am the best horseman. If there is someone over there, they probably won't speak German and I am multilingual. I am the one most suited to do the job. I can leave right away. At first there are objections but after a brief debate, when all things are considered, Sophia is right She is the best person to go for help. I am so worried about her riding alone.

Fritz makes a hackamore bridle out of rope and I put a blanket on the horse's back. Sophia points up the mountain side and screams "Indians! There are about thirty Indians looking down at us. What else? Without powder, we don't even have a weapon to defend ourselves!"

Someone calls out, "Women and children get behind the wagons!"

The Indians begin coming down at us. Our powder is wet so we will be using our muskets a club. Get ready!

As they get closer, I can see that they aren't carrying weapons. They are mainly women and children that are carrying bowls and large gourds. They're smiling and laughing and talking to us in their native language. As they are entering camp, the women are carrying the bowls and are offering them to us.

I look up at Sophia who is mounted on the horse. She looks down at me and after a moment's pause, a smile forms on her face that turns into a laugh. We are looking at each other and laughing uncontrollably. "We will survive!"

I welcome our new guests into our camp with arm gestures and a smile. Fritz calls out, "Come out from behind the wagon's ladies! Come out and meet our guests!"

The Indians have brought large bowls containing what appears to be a cold corn soup for us. It's apparent that our Native American guests are happy to be able to help us. Sophia dismounts and graciously invites our new friends to sit with us. We wasted no time in getting cups and began eating. One of the women that's with our guests has blue eyes and can speak some broken English. She was probably captured by the tribe in her youth. Sophia speaks English so she is our interpreter.

Our guests explain that they belong to the Lenni Lenape tribe. The woman Sophia is talking to is "Nitkuxkwike."

She tells Sophia that her name means "Blue eyes wide open." Nitkuxkwike tells Sophia that her village is located nearby on a plateau. They had been watching us for days. They say, "Our foolishness was comedic."

"We think you are all "witko." Sophia asks, "what is witko?"

"Crazy" Nitkuxkwike answers, only a fool would choose to camp next to a flooding river. And have the door of their tent face upstream."

Nitkuxkwike goes on to say that when she was young, her tribe was told by US soldiers to move west to the Indiana Territory. Her family and group of other Lenni Lenape defied the Army's orders and stayed here on their homeland. They have been evading the Army ever since. We ate well and spend the remainder of the day joking and laughing at ourselves with our new friends. They had been watching while we were going through our turmoil. These people had been through many hard ships and know what it is like. They are doing what they can to help us survive. The Lenni Lenape people are truly generous and forgiving people. Europeans that I have known would be bitter if they had been treated the way these Lenni Lenape people had been.

It's getting dark now and without saying a word our friends gather their belongings. As we say good-bye, I'm thinking how fortunate we are to have met Nitkuxkwike and her neighbors. They saved our lives and would not even accept any payment or even a thank you for it.

It's morning and the sun is peeking over the mountains.

Hans addresses all of us. He tells us that he and his wife, Anita has decided to remain here. In anticipation of our objecting to his choice, he asks us not to try to talk them out of their decision. He says, "Our family is here, and here is where we will remain. We all understand and respect Hans and Anita's decision. I understand completely. It will be a lonely and dangerous existence. Although pilgrims heading west will pass by on occasion. I'm sure that our friends, the Lenni Lenape will check on them from time to time as well.

The next few days are relatively uneventful. We climb six mountain ranges. Each mountain range is lower than the one before it. Each valley is wider than the one before it. Today, we are seeing a few farms. An Irish farmer that we pass, tells Sophia that a city named Pittsburgh is twenty miles ahead of us. When

Sophia asks about lodging, he tells her that there is a hotel five miles up the trail. Sophia and I agree that it would be nice to stay in a hotel tonight.

When we arrive at the hotel, we find that the innkeeper is Swiss, and he speaks German. It is a different dialect than I speak but I can understand most of what he is saying. It's refreshing to be able understand someone speaking other than our own party. Sophia and I treat ourselves to a private room and a meal in the hotel restaurant. Such luxury!

After dinner, I order a couple of steins of ale. We go upstairs to the front balcony. There, we find a bench so we sit down. We hold our mugs up. Sophia toasts to our love for each other and to a safe journey to Wisconsin. I think to myself, "Wow, that is the first time she has ever said the word love!"

I'm looking at Sophia and I see the most beautiful person I have ever met. I ask, "Sophia, why did a smart, loving person like you choose a common peasant like me? You could have had any wealthy person you wanted."

She smiles and turns toward me, then she puts her hand on mine. You're right, I could have had any man, and I chose you. Then she punches me in the arm and laughs.

Chapter Seven

Gateway to the West

Sophia and I wake up to the smell of smoke. I walk out on the deck to see smoke coming from the north. Sophia follows me. She rests her hand on my shoulder and asks, "What now?"

I answer, "I'll talk to the innkeeper. He may be able to tell me something about the fire.

We go downstairs to get a couple of biscuits and sausage for breakfast. I ask the cook about the fire. He responds, "Fire? Is there a fire? I haven't heard anything about a fire."

"The smoke, don't you smell the smoke?" I ask.

"No." He answers.

I point to the North. "Look out the window!"

"Oh that. That's just Pittsburgh. The wind must be from the north this morning. It's the steel mills, factories, and foundries."

Fritz and his family are waiting for us outside the hotel. I get our cart from the hotel's barn, and we are on our way. Next stop Pittsburgh! Sophia and I are talking about sleeping in a bed last night. We had the best night's sleep since we were in Baltimore. I am well rested, and we are walking at a fast pace today.

We are approaching a sign Sophia says, "Pittsburgh five miles."

I'm looking forward to seeing the city. I can smell the prosperity from five miles away. I'm wondering, what makes Pittsburgh such a busy place?

Pittsburgh, Pennsylvania in 1830 *

Geographically located where the Monongahela and Allegheny Rivers meet to form the headwaters of the Ohio River. This makes shipping to the Midwestern states and beyond possible.

The city of Pittsburgh is located in the middle of one of the most prolific coalfields in America. The region is also rich in iron ore, brass, tin and, petroleum. Limestone, used in the smelting process of iron ore, is readily available in the area as well.

At this point, manufacturing has overtaken commerce as the mainstay in Pittsburgh's economy. It will soon rival Birmingham, Boston, and Baltimore as America's leader in manufacturing. At least thirty iron ore processing companies exist in the city at this time. Most of them have two or more blast furnaces for processing iron. Each furnace is given a woman's name. Newspapers are calling Pittsburgh "The Iron City"

Hundreds of companies that are employing thousands of workers that make products of iron have sprung up. Products such as nails, frying pans, barrel straps, hinges, and kettles are produced.

Events in the previous two decades were critical in Pittsburgh's growth. In 1811 the first steamboat was built in Pittsburgh. Steamboats allowed commerce to travel upriver for the first time. The War of 1812 catalyzed growth in The Iron City. When the British cut-off trade of iron and steel products to the United States inland commerce increased. Pittsburgh was in a position to provide products to Americans that replaced British goods. By 1815 Pittsburgh was producing $764K in iron, $249K in brass and tin. It produced $235K in glass products. There was a constant cloud of coal dust hanging over the city. The residents didn't mind the dust because it represents a sign of prosperity!

* Wikipedia

Pittsburgh, Pennsylvania

"This city is amazing. There is so much opportunity!" I proclaim. I'm seeing new manufacturing buildings being built and the existing plants are having additions built onto them. New homes are being built everywhere. There are also several shipyards along the river that are building steamboats.

"Workers wanted" signs are in front of most factories, and they are printed in as many as six languages. I didn't know it at the time, but I was witnessing the time and birthplace of the American industrial revolution. This is the beginning of what will be prosperity in America for the next 200 years.

Sophia and I find a bench in front of a barber shop and we sit down. "Sophia, could this be our new home?" I ask. I go on to say, "There are many good-paying jobs here. Perhaps someday I could start my own business here. We could save our money and buy a house. Could this be the city where we raise our children?"

Sophia pauses for a moment and then responds, "If this is the place you choose to live, then I will stay here with you. If you want to buy a house here, then I will make it our home. Consider this, we have come this far following your dream. Your vision was to go to Wisconsin and have land of your own." She goes on to say, "You have come this far to find a better life. I have come this far to flee my old life. At this point, I have come far enough to escape my other life. So, the only question is, have you reached your dream?"

There is so much to process. I'm confident that in this burgeoning city, even common laborers are making wages that can afford nice houses and fine buggies. I could reach financial goals well beyond anything that I could have ever imagined. I look up to the sky. I can't see the sun. It's hidden up there somewhere behind the black smoke. My throat stings from the acidic air and I have listened to Sophia coughing all morning. "Sophia, we are burning daylight." I stand up and point west. "Wisconsin is that way."

Chapter Eight

Tecumseh

We meet with Fritz at the hotel where he and his family stayed last night. "When would you like to head out, Fritz?" He looks me in the eye and responds, "Johann, I've decided that we will stay here in Pittsburgh."

I give him an understanding nod and speak. "I understand. I'll miss you, my friend. If you get to Wisconsin, make sure to look me up."

Sophia steps forward and gives Fritz a hug goodbye and an understanding smile. There is nothing more to be said so we turn and walk out the door. I'm thinking, about how Fritz and I have been through so much in our short acquaintance. I'll truly miss that man. I hope to see him again someday Many of the men in our group chose to stay in Pittsburgh as well.

When we are checking out of the hotel, I ask the Innkeeper, "I'm going west to Wisconsin Territory. How do I get to the Great Lakes Trail?"

He counts my change and then says, "The Great Lakes Trail begins at Harper's landing. You will want to take a steamboat down the Ohio River to Harper's Landing. It takes a day to get there. You will find pilgrims that are going into the frontier gathering at Harper's Landing. It would be wise to go into the wilderness with a group.

We board a steamboat and are bound for East Liverpool, Ohio. The Caption tells me that the trip will take ten hours. On the way down the river, we are seeing many Indian villages. When I ask, one of the ship's crewmen, he tells me that they are of either of the Ottawa, Shawne, or Miami tribes.

I ask, "are any of those tribes on the warpath?"

The crewman chuckles, "I haven't heard of any trouble with the Indians in these parts for years."

I hear the ship's bell ring five times indicating that it's five o'clock in the afternoon. The boat whistle now sounds, and the boat is slowing as we pull into the dock at Harper's Landing. It appears to be a little village with about one hundred people. There is a hotel in the village, but we will camp behind the hotel with some of the other travelers to save money. The fee to camp and have use of the pump and outhouse is four cents. Nine other families are camping behind the hotel boo. They are traveling west on the Great Lakes Trail and are waiting for more people to travel with them. Seven of the family's mule or horse-drawn wagons, the rest have carts like I have. Four of the families are German speaking, four are Poles and there are two Irish families. Sophia speaks Polish and English and has introduced herself to everyone.

She set up a meeting around the campfire for this evening to talk about when we will leave to go west.

Sophia began the meeting by saying in German, by saying that she will be happy to be the interpreter. Then she repeated it in Polish and then in English There are nods, indicating an agreement to her proposal. With that, the meeting begins. We are discussing a variety of issues. The meeting ends when we agree that we will leave in the morning.

Our journey across Ohio has begun. The plan is that we will continue traveling on the Great Lakes Trail across the state.

At this time, Ohio has been a state for seventeen years. With the exception of it's capital, Columbus, most of the people in this state live along Lake Erie and the Ohio River. The interior is, for the most part, wilderness.

The first two days in Ohio are uneventful. The terrain is hilly but far better than walking in the mountains that we had encountered in Pennsylvania. Homesteaders that we have passed have warned us to beware of Tecumseh. They are telling us that Tecumseh is a Shawnee chief who opposes white settlers taking over tribal lands. The chief is creating a coalition among many of the native tribes. He and his allies have been harassing settlers from Ohio to the Mississippi river and Canada south to the gulf coast.

The chief believes, like most Indians, that land was like the air and water. It is a common possession of all Indians. We are told that Shawnee war chiefs, Blue Jacket and Tecumseh recently led a war party against Army General Arthur St. Claire at the battle of Wabash, in Indiana. Nine hundred and fifty-two of St. Claire's one thousand troops were killed. *

The Indian coalition has been raiding farms and villages throughout the frontier. Merciless attacks have been reported along the Great Lakes Trail. I am hearing that Indians are killing and disfiguring pioneer men and capturing the women.

We are now three days away from the safety of Fort Hayes. The terrain around us is heavily wooded with towering virgin hardwoods. The girth of these trees are wide enough that Indians could be hiding behind many of them. Occasionally a dog will bark an alarm and the men will grab their muskets. Thankfully, we have not encountered any Redskins yet. I have never felt this much stress in my life. Sophia on the other hand, seems to be handling the tension quite well. She is my iron lady.

It's day three in Ohio. The Indian scare has caused most of the farmers to abandon their homesteads and go to the nearest town for protection. Indians are pilfering and burning the abandoned properties. Some whites are using this opportunity to steal from their neighbors and blaming it on the Redskins.

* Wikipedia

Tecumseh

Born near Cincinnati, Tecumseh's father was killed by whites at an early age. His mother was of the Muskogee tribe. She instilled in him a hate for white men. At seven, Tecumseh's mother left him to be reared by his older sister and they moved to Missouri. He and his sister lived with the Shawnee and were trained in their strict moral code of honesty. He was adopted by Shawnee Chief, Blackfish, and grew into manhood with two white stepbrothers whom Blackfish had captured.

The invasion of Shawnee lands, burning of their crops, and murder of his people intensified the hatred of whites that his mother had instilled in him. At the age of fourteen Tecumseh and his father joined in one of the predatory raids on flat boats that were carrying whites into Shawnee lands on the Ohio River.

Tecumseh spent the rest of his life resisting the Whiteman's invasion of Indian lands. Over time he became a leader in his cause. Tecumseh recruited tribes all across the western frontier, from Ontario to Alabama promoting his Indian resistance movement.

He developed oratory, that whites compared to Henry Clay. His persuasive skills created alliances between tribes for his cause throughout the west. *

* Wikipedia

We are seeing evidence that other pioneers had been attacked on the trail recently.

One of the Irishmen traveling with us, named Abraham is a retired sergeant in the US Army. He has fought Indians who were British allies in the War of 1812. Abraham has taken command of our defense and we are glad to have him. He is the only one of us that has any experience in warfare.

The forest had been logged in this area about ten years ago. The underbrush that has grown replacing the tall trees is thick and an enemy can easily hide in it.

Abraham addresses us, "Men, most of the Indians will have muskets. The rest will have bows and arrows. Frankly, in my opinion, the bows are my greater concern, because they are repeating weapons. Shawnee braves can shoot twenty arrows in the time it takes his enemy to reload his musket. When under attack, hold your fire until you are certain that you will hit your target. The enemy's favorite tactic will be to have us shoot early and emptying our weapons. They will then attack, firing their weapons at a closer and more accurate range. Be prepared to have the Shawnee rush us, yelling and screaming in an effort to put fear and confusion in us. Each warrior will have a club with a heavy stone attached to end or a tomahawk. They will swing for your head. If they make contact, it is instantly fatal. A blow to the body is disabling. In hand-to-hand combat, strike first and strike hard."

"Our enemy has trained for battle all their lives. He is skilled and experienced in warfare. In the mind of the Shawnee, we are the invading enemy. And we truly are. They hate us with all of their being and that gives them strength."

Abraham continues, "So you see, our adversary has all the advantages. Be vigilant, be brave. God willing, we will get through this."

Abraham told each of the men to have a hand weapon such as a hatchet, ax, or club at his side at all times.

Every step we take is one step closer to the safety of Fort Hayes. Sophia is insisting on pulling our cart so that I can have both hands on my musket. I can see that she is straining and exhausted but won't say a word. Sophia is telling me that she wants to buy a musket and learn how to shoot it when we get to Fort Hayes. Hopefully, she will change her mind.

The terrain has changed from hills that we had yesterday, to flatter land today. There are streams and rivers. The forest has virgin hardwood trees. The trees are as high as ninety feet. The trunks of the trees are as wide as six feet in diameter.

Very little light is able to penetrate the canopy, The ground is carpeted with ferns that are about two feet tall.

The driver of the lead wagon cries out, "A wagoy prixadr odunami! Wagoy prixedr nami!"

I look at Sophia and ask What's he saying?"

Sophia responds, "I think he's saying something about a wagon. Maybe, wagons ahead?"

Our caravan stops. Abraham jogs up to the front of the caravan to see what's going on. When he gets there, he calls back to us, "There are wagons in the trail"

I think to myself, "How could that be? The caravan that is traveling on this trail ahead of us, left over a week before we did, how could we have caught up with them?"

As we get closer to the wagons, we see that there is no one around. "This doesn't look good."

We clinch our guns tight and approach slowly with apprehension. The wagons are in the in the trail but the horses and oxen that had pulled them are gone. It smells like rotten eggs. Now I see dead and bloating bodies everywhere. It was a massacre! Bodies had been dismembered. There are signs that men had been tortured in front of their families before they died. This is hideous.

Someone calls out, "Women keep the children away!"

After the initial shock of this inhumanity a consuming paranoia overcomes me. I feel like there are Indians all around us. I then think to myself, keep calm Johann, get a hold of yourself. All of this happened a week ago.

Sophia asks me, "Johann, do you see any women or children? Where are the women and children?"

Abraham overhears Sophia's question and answers in a quiet, sober voice, "They took them. The Shawnee will keep them as slaves or sell them to other tribes. If a warrior decides that he likes one of the boys he may adopt him as his son."

The question that we all have is, what do we do with the bodies? One of the Irishmen speaks first. "We have to give them a Christian burial."

The other Irishman quickly responds, "That will take the rest of the day. It will be dark before we finish burying them. We don't have time for that. We must keep moving and get as close to the fort as we can before dark. We don't know, Shawnee warriors may be nearby us right now!"

A debate goes on for a few minutes and then Petrus, from Saxony suggests, "Let's vote on it. All of you men that are in favor of burying the bodies before we leave raise your hand." A clear majority votes to leave this place.

Abraham addresses us, "Okay, let's get moving, I'll report this massacre to the general in command at Fort Hayes when we get there. Now let's get moving. Like one of you said, the Shawnee could be nearby."

God blesses us with his protection, and we arrive at Fort Hayes safely at dusk. There is a small town that had built up around the fort with a post office, general store, and a few saloons. Some of the town's people came out to greet us. They are clearly worried about Chief Tecumseh's war.

Two of the saloons have rooms for rent so Sophia and I decide to stay in one of them.

After dinner, I buy a jug of beer at the bar and grab a couple of tin cups. Then Sophia and I sit down on the balcony outside of our room. For the moment we are out of danger. I pour a cup of beer for each of us. We toast to the soles of the victims that were massacred, then take a drink. This is our first opportunity to be alone since we were in Pittsburgh. Sophia playfully punches me in the arm and she laughs.

I say, "You haven't laughed like this in almost a week. It makes me happy so see you laugh."

Then I think to myself that the next leg of our trip in Indiana promises to be more dangerous than Ohio. Sophia is quiet too. I wonder if she is thinking what I am. I look at her and I'm seeing my beautiful Sophia. We have both changed since we began this trip. I remember the soft, manicured hands and clean complexion that she had when we met in the stable. She now has calluses on her hands and dirt under her fingernails. Her face and arms are tan for the first time in her life.

Tomorrow we will be entering Indiana Territory. A group of eleven families that are camping outside the gate here at Fort

Hayes will be joining us. We were hoping that we would be escorted by soldiers through Indiana but that has changed. A Captain informed us that he was given orders to go to Northern Ohio to intervene in a border conflict between the State of Ohio and Michigan Territory.

Toledo War *

Nineteenth-century surveying errors and mapping mistakes led the governments of Michigan and Ohio to both claim jurisdiction of a 468 square mile region along their border. The situation came to a head when Michigan petitioned for statehood

Both Michigan and Ohio called up their state militia. The two forces were deployed on opposite sides of the Maumee River west of Toledo.

The United States federal government stepped in to mediate and offered Michigan the Upper Peninsula, which was part of was part of Wisconsin Territory consisting of nine thousand square miles in exchange for the 468 square mile Toledo strip.

During this time, Indiana, whose northern border was south of Lake Michigan saw the benefits of having a port city on Lake Michigan. Indiana took ten miles from Michigan's Southern border. Michigan then went to war with Indiana. Illinois, after seeing Indiana's land grab, for port cities, took land from Wisconsin Territory that extended from the southern point of Lake Michigan, north to the Indian village of Waukegan. (Michigan went to war with Ohio and Wisconsin lost.)

---

* Wikipedia

Sophia and I are awake at first light this morning. The plan is to rendezvous with the other group of travelers near the fort gate at seven a.m. Our destination today is Fort Wayne, in Indiana.

The other travelers begin gathering an hour after sunrise. Sophia and I are among the earliest. It gives us a chance to meet some of our new traveling companions. The other group is from Poland. The Poles had been Mecklenburg's enemy for over one hundred years. Here, that bitter history between our people doesn't exist among us. We are all just Americans looking forward to the future in our new country. The Polish group is going to Fort Dearborn. They tell Sophia that the fort is located where the Chicago River meets Lake Michigan in Illinois.

We are getting the caravan organized to leave and it is taking some time. There is a spirit of cooperation, but the different languages it is making this task difficult. The general store is opening so Sophia, (the only one of us that can translate our languages) is walking over there to buy some items that we will need such as flour, salt, beets, and potatoes.

We are ready to start out. I look over to the general store wondering what happened to Sophia. What is taking her so long? okay, there she is. She is coming out of the store and walking toward me. She's carrying the salt, flour, beets, potatoes, and a musket? I should have expected that she would buy one. She did tell me that she was going to.

Chapter Nine

Indiana, "Land of Indians"

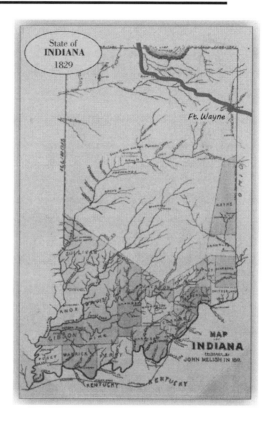

The state of Indiana petitioned for and was granted statehood in 1816. In the 1830 census the population is 343,000. It's said that 90% of the population is within forty miles of the Ohio and Wabash rivers. The state has grown more than 150% in the past ten years. The Northern part of Indiana is a vast wilderness populated by the Miami, Illinois, Potawatomi, Shawnee, and other smaller Indian tribes. *

* Wikipedia

I find myself back on cart pulling duty this morning as Sophia is carrying her new musket. The owner of the general store showed her how to load the gun, so it's loaded. A woman carrying a musket is remarkably odd and our new friends in this caravan haven't seen it before. There is a lot of whispering and pointing at Sophia going on this morning. They think a woman having a gun is strange. Frankly, I think it's dangerous!

The terrain here in Indiana is like the densely wooded hills of western Ohio. Except lately the terrain is becoming a little flatter. We are all well rested, so we are traveling until sundown today. One of the officers back at the fort told us that we will find small rivers and lakes along the trail for campsites with water at the end of the day.

A Lieutenant at the fort told us that an Indian threat exists. He went on to tell us that to address the "Indian Problem" the United States Congress passed The Indian Removal Act in March of this year. Congress ordered the Army to remove all the Indians from the western frontier territories and send them west of the Mississippi River. Indians that are living on reservations are included in the removal. Reservation lands will be taken over by the US Government and sold to white settlers. As much as I want to have cheap land in America, this act seems grossly unfair to me. I'm thinking of the peaceful Indian villages that we passed on the Ohio River. Those people may have been living there for generations. What kind of government would do this to their citizens?

As I think back to hearing the Lieutenant saying, "There have been ambushes on the trail all across the territory."

He went on to say that, "In the years that he has served at Fort Wayne, he had never seen the Shawnee attack unless they were confident of an overwhelming victory."

This Spring, under the authority of the United States Congress's Indian Removal Act, General Scott and seven thousand troops that serve under his command, are removing all the Indians from there their homes and escorting them west of the Mississippi River.

Word of this atrocity is traveling among the Indian tribes. Shawnee chief Tecumseh is taking a leadership role among the tribes. He is traveling across the frontier promoting a united resistance against the white men that are invading their lands. He is a talented auditor. He is known for saying, "One twig will break but a bundle of twigs are strong. We must unite." A chief from the Fox tribe in western Wisconsin Territory named Black Hawk, has declared war on all white men. He is leading a band of Fox and Sauk warriors that are raiding white men's farms and villages in southern Wisconsin and northern Illinois. It is reported that at this point he has attacked and raided over one hundred white homesteads and settlements.

We have thirty armed men (and one-armed woman) in our wagon train. I see fear in the faces of men and women. The children can sense the stress that we are under, and they are terrified. We are tradesmen and farmers; we aren't soldiers and warriors. I worry that the Indians know it. I'm sure that they do.

This land in Indiana is vast and beautiful with wild game of all kinds all around us. I see no reason why the White men and Redskins can't find a way to share this amazing country.

We are looking at a herd of buffalo! They are magnificent beasts. Four of us decide to go over to them and shoot one for camp meat. This is exciting for me. I have never shot an animal before or anything else other than a paper target for that matter. One of the Poles has some experience as a butcher, so he is coming along with us. There are about 20 buffalo in the herd, and they're grazing in a clearing about one hundred paces away.

The plan is that we separate into pairs and sneak up until we get into shooting range. Two of us are walking slowly and quietly to the right and two to the left. The buffalo start snorting in an agitated way as soon as they see us separate. I think, "These animals have been watching us. They know that we are becoming a threat." I signal the others to be quiet and get down and out of sight. We stay still, for a few minutes until the beasts settle down. Now, we're crawling slowly toward them on our bellies in the tall grass.

We've been slowly creeping with our heads down for what seems like about ten minutes. We haven't been able to see the brutes since we began crawling. I'm thinking that maybe they walked away. So, I slowly raise my head to look. There's one, he's just twenty or thirty steps away from me! He snorts a warning. I think he saw me. Several others start grunting and snorting all around us. We crawled right in the middle of the herd! I slowly put my gun up to my shoulder. He is still standing there motionless. I slowly pull the hammer back until it locks.

≈Click ≈ the whole damn herd takes off running in all directions! I take aim at his heart and notice another bison running straight at me. I swing on the onrushing bull, aim in the center of his enormous head and fire. Click ≈**Bang!**≈

He disappears behind the muzzle smoke for a moment. Then, I hear pounding hooves. The one-ton beast is running through the smoke right past me, just an arm's length away! I quickly swing around to watch him to see him running through the smoke and dust. He stumbles, goes down and rolls in a billow of dust. I swear that I can feel the earth shake when he hit the ground.

I sit up and turn toward the buffalo fearing that he might somehow get up. I'm breathing hard and I can feel my heart pounding. I take a deep breath and exhale. I try to stand up but my legs are shaking so I drop down to my knees. I pause for a while to get control of my emotions. I'm looking at that magnificent animal. He's lying on his side, motionless. He inhales one last time, holds onto it as long as he can, somehow knowing that it is his last. Then a long exhale, as if he is returning the air to this earth that has provided life for him all of his years. And now, he is lifeless.

A feeling of remorse overtakes me as I look into his lifeless eye, staring into the sky. How could I have done this?

Stephan, who was stalking the buffalo with me, senses how I'm feeling. He walks up to me and says, "This buffalo will feed all our people for a week.

Good job." I think to myself, "Yes it will. It was put on this earth to serve us."

The caravan kept moving on while we were hunting. One wagon was left behind with us hunters to carry the buffalo meat.

The Polish butcher named Janusz drives the wagon over to us.

He climbs down from the driver's seat and then gets his box of skinning knives, carving knives and bone saw out of the back of the wagon.

He then says, "Czy ktosniej oskorowal woku? (Has anyone skinned an ox before?)

We look at each other as if to say, "Does anyone know what he is saying?"

Janusz motions to us while speaking in polish and begins showing us how to sin and butcher the buffalo. It took more than three hours to process the meat and load it on the wagon.

We're now traveling alone trying to catch up with the caravan. If the Shawnee didn't know that we were here before. Any warrior within a mile heard the shot and they know exactly where we are now. The Indians think of the buffalo as we think of our cattle. From the Indians' point of view, we are stealing their property. The buffalo sustains their lives. The penalty for taking their buffalo is death.

When we rejoin our group, they have already set up camp for the evening. We are all going to be dining on prime cuts of buffalo tonight!

Agnieszka and Tomasz Plutowski and their children are a family that is traveling with us. Because Sophia speaks Polish, she has gotten to know Agnieszka, her husband, and children quite well. Sophia told me that she will be traveling with Agnieska today because one of her children, five-year- old Nikola, had become quite sick last night. She is vomiting and has violent diarrhea.

We are traveling through an area that has had several Indian raids on settlers, so we are on high alert. We are approaching a little town that was abandoned because of the Indian scare. It was a Polish immigrant community. The village is named

Warsaw, it's nestled among five small lakes and the Tippecanoe River. The river powered a sawmill and a grist mill. There was a general store, several saloons and about thirty houses. I can see farms surrounding the little town. All are completely abandoned.

There was a bridge in this little town, but it was destroyed so we will need to portage the River. Portaging rivers is something we do daily. It has become a routine, but it can be dangerous, so we take it seriously. Recent heavy rain up stream has put the river at a high level and the water is running fast. The carts and Conestoga wagons are built to be somewhat watertight, giving them the ability to float for a while.

We always take the carts across the river before the Conestoga wagons. On shallower rivers and slow-moving water, I can take my cart across by myself. This river is fast moving, and the depth is four feet on the far shore. It will require three men to take each cart across the river. As a precaution we tie ropes to the to the carts and have men on each shore holding on to them.

After the carts are across the river, we bring on the covered wagons. The horses have crossed many rivers before but never one as deep and fast moving as this one

Mikola Dabrowski is our most skilled teamster, and he has his team of horses very well trained, so he is always the first to cross the rivers. The rest of the wagons follow with thirty to forty feet between each wagon. River crossing is a slow process, and it can be dangerous. Some horses are spooking as they cross the river, so it is a challenge for the drivers to keep them under control.

The water is deeper on the far side of the river and some of the wagons are beginning to float in the deep water. This the first time that we are crossing a river that is deep enough for the wagons to float and for the most part the horses are handling it well. This is a tense process, and as each wagon reaches the far shore, I'm feeling a little more relieved. The horses are getting better at these crossings and the drivers are becoming more skilled at the process. As Alrick Eichmann's is crossing his wagon begins to float in the deep water. The horses spook and the wagon comes to a sudden stop causing Alrick to fall forward onto one of his horse's butt. The horse begins kicking. Alrick slips down behind the horse into the thrashing water. He gets hung up on the wagon's front wheel. The wagon begins floating and swings downstream with the current allowing Alrick to get free from the wheel.

I'm waiting for Alrick to swim up from under his wagon, but he isn't coming up. Then his motionless body rises to the surface about ten feet downstream. He's floating in the current face down. Two men immediately jump into the river and swim to Alrick. By the time they get to him, Alrick has floated about thirty yards downstream in the fast-moving current.

While they are swimming to Alrick, I jump into the water and swim to his wagon. The wagon is drifting downstream too. The horses are swimming with the current. I'm swimming as hard

as I can, trying to catch up to the wagon. The water is so cold. Wearing these heavy clothes and boots is making swimming hard. I'm at the wagon now. I am so tired. I use the last of my strength to climb onto the driver's seat. I take a little time, but I'm able to calm the horses and drive them to shore.

Alrick is brought to shore. Tragically, he died from his horses kicking him in his head. He left behind, his wife Gretchen and seven young children, who were in the wagon and witnessed the event.

We buried Alrick in the village graveyard, located behind the church. After burying Alrick, it is getting late so the men in our group meet together and decided that we will spend the night here in this little ghost town.

I wake up before first light this morning to rain on the tent. We are going to try to make up some of the time that we lost yesterday crossing the river and burying poor Alrick. I tie my cart to the back of Alrick's wagon. I'll drive Alrick's wagon and Sophia is going to ride in the wagon with Gretchen and her children this morning. Mikola and his wife will take over for us in the afternoon.

Sophia and I are walking on the trail side by side pulling our cart this afternoon. We are both deep in thought and haven't spoken in quite a while. I'm thinking of how our wagon train, consisting of a group of people that had never even seen each other a week ago, has become a family of sorts. We came from two countries that had been at war on and off for one hundred years. Our people had considered the Poles to be dreadful enemies. But, like me, none of us Mecklenburgers had ever met a Polish person before. Most of us have relatives that had met the Poles on the battlefield in years past. We have now learned that we have so much in common with the poles. I'm pleasantly surprised at their friendly nature and generosity.

I must say, that there was some distrust among us in the beginning. Our different languages were an issue for a while, but we quickly found that there are so many similarities in our languages that we were able to communicate fairly well.

I must chuckle when I think of the polish jokes that we used to say. The jokes always depicted the Pollock as being stupid and foolish. That portrayal couldn't be farther from the truth. The Poles we are traveling with are smart, hardworking, and dedicated to their family and friends. I think I can trust my life to those men when the time comes. I know they can count on me to fight for them and their families when the chips are down. If the time comes, I will be proud to fight next to my new friends if it's required.

The vomiting and diarrhea have gotten worse for little Nikola. Now his mother and his other six siblings are showing the same symptoms. I see that his father, Tomasz has diarrhea and stomach pain too but won't admit it. Thomasz is too weak to drive his wagon. Other men and Women are taking the reins for him so that Thomasz can lay down in the wagon with the rest of his family. The youngest two children that were the first to show mild symptoms are now noticeably losing weight. Some of the other children in our group are beginning to show symptoms of cholera.

> *Cholera is an infectious disease caused by a bacterium called Vibrio cholera. The bacteria typically live in warm water. Cholera causes severe diarrhea and dehydration. A cholera pandemic began in the US in 1829. It caused over 150,000 deaths.*
>
> *Today, Cholera infections are rare in industrialized nations. Modern sewage and water sanitization, early testing and treatment has virtually eliminated the disease. **

I hope that his will be our last evening in Indiana. Tonight, we are camping at the crossroads of an ancient Indian trail named the "Sauk Trail." The Sauk Trail is a foot path that runs between Rock Island, Illinois and Fort Detroit. A Potawatomi village named Chiqua is located here. This trail intersection has created a natural trading place. It's kind of the commercial center for the Potawatomi nation and other smaller tribes in the region. The tribes in the area have decided that this will be a free enterprise zone and they will allow all tribes and races to come and go without being harassed. Furthermore, they provide some degree of protection to all travelers in this area to encourage traders to do business in Chiqua.

I sit down next to an old trapper that is sitting on a bench outside the barber shop. He is telling me that, local tribes have been living here and trading for hundreds of years. Many years ago the French located a Hudson's Bay Company trading post here. Then, after the British won control of this area in 1763, an English trading post was built here. The British allowed the Hudson's Bay Company to continue operating here. Americans have four trading posts here as well. Chiqua is truly a sanctum of international commerce.

* Mayo Clinic

*Potawatomi Chiefs will sell Chiqua including the land surrounding Chiqua to the US Government in 1832 causing a chain of events. All Indians will be forced to move west, across the Mississippi River. The trading posts will eventually go out of business. They will close and will move out. Chief Tecumseh will be known for saying; "The chiefs were drunk when they sold our land." **

* Wikipedia

Chapter Ten

Fort Dearborn

We will be leaving the relative safety of the Chique zone early today and then moving onto Illinois. We were told to be aware of a chief of the Fox tribe named Black Hawk. He and his warriors are raiding homesteads and frontier villages in northern Illinois and southern Wisconsin. Traveling homesteaders are one of his favorite targets.

Little Nikola lost to his battle with cholera this morning. His father Tomasz and his entire family continue suffering from the disease. Tomasz looks like he's lost forty pounds, and like the rest of his family, has not been able to get out of his bedroll in their wagon. Sophia and some of the other women have been taking care of the family. She is particularly worried about seven-year-old Natalia.

Tonight, Sophia is watching over Tomasz and his family. Natalia has a high fever and is shivering. Sophia goes to her and holds Natalia tight and begins rocking her gently. Natalia slowly opens her blue eyes and looks up at Sophia.

In a weak voice, quietly says, "Sophie, I love you. Thank you for taking care of me. Can I kiss you good-bye? I'm going away to see Nikola tonight. He told me that he is waiting for Daddy and me." Sophia accepted Natalia's kiss, with tears in her eyes, kissed her back and hugs her tight.

Tomasz and young Natalia died in the night. We buried them along the trail this morning and continued on our way.

Chief Black Hawk
B. 1767 D. 1838

Black Hawk is a member of the Mesquaki (Fox) tribe. The Fox tribal lands are located near the Mississippi River along the Wisconsin and Illinois boarder. Determined to resist the growing presence of white settlers on tribal lands, Chief, Black Hawk declared war on the US Government. Black Hawk and his warriors had an estimated one hundred and fifty battles, skirmishes and raids before he surrendered to General Atkinson.*

* Wisconsin Historical Society

Under authority of the Indian removal act, The United States Army escorted members of the Fox tribe from their tribal lands in Illinois to the west side of the Mississippi River. In April of this year fifteen hundred Fox Indians crossed the Mississippi and went back to their old cornfields and hunting grounds on their tribal lands in Illinois.

Major Isaiah Stallman and 275 Illinois militia attempted to move the tribe back to Iowa. Black Hawk and his warriors attacked the Illinois militia. When confronted by Black Hawk, and his warriors the Major and his militia panicked and ran. And so, the Black Hawk War began.

With his newfound determination and confidence to resist the growing presence of white settlers. Black Hawk and his warriors have been raiding farms and villages. He is also winning significant victories against the Wisconsin and Illinois militia. Settlers in the area in a state of panic. Warriors from the Potawatomi, and Ho-Chunk tribes are joining him now.

Major General Edmond P. Gaines ordered Brigadier General Samuel Whiteside and Brigadier General Henry Atkinson along with 2500 Army officers and enlisted troops serving under them, to hunt down Black Hawk and his warriors. When captured, they are to escort them back to the west of the Mississippi River.

Our caravan is getting close to the Illinois border. The Poles that are traveling with us intend to settle in the Village of Chicago. One of the Poles named George Walker has become a good friend of mine during our time together on this trail. George is asking me to consider Chicago as our new home. Solomon Juneau, a fur trader that joined us in Cuiqua speaks up and says, "Milwaukee is where the opportunities are. Chicago is just a very small, struggling village. I have a fur trading business in Milwaukee. I'm looking for help Johann, if you need a job when you get to Milwaukee look me up. My trading post is on Jauk Trail near the Court House. My name is on the building.

We are traveling through a forest of towering oak and hickory trees. These trees are huge. They stand 70 feet tall and some of them have a ten-foot girth. Very little light is permeating the canopy above us. The ground is damp and has a carpet of moss on it. There is a lifeless silence. The only sound being heard is a squeaky wagon wheel. The air is cool and moist. The wind is not able penetrate the forest canopy.

Birds begin chattering warnings in the trees at a distance on my left us. They are announcing the presence of a predator. Walker's dog starts growling then puts his nose up in the air sniffing with quick, short breaths. Lowering his head, I watch him scan the forest with an absolute focus. He's looking through the trees for the slightest movement. I see him take three quick steps forward, then freeze.

He begins growling again. "George, check your dog. He senses something out there... Shhhh, quiet!

"George look to your left. There is a fern moving about eighty paces out on your left It could be an animal or, it could be Indians. You walk along the train toward the back and alert everyone. I'll walk to the front and do the same. Abraham is at the front. I'll let him know what we saw. If its Indians don't let them know that we are aware that they are out there."

When I talk to Abraham and show him where the movement was. Abraham orders in a commanding tone, "Stop the wagons! The enemy is to the left! Children, get in the wagons. Unhitch the horses!"

The Indians now know that they've been spotted. Now there is obvious movement in the forest. Someone calls out. "Look, they're behind us too!"

Abraham orders. "Men, get under the wagons and get ready!" Sophia and I crawl under a wagon. Suddenly, it's silent except for the dogs that are sensing the tension and are barking.

Sophia and I are laying down side by side under a wagon with our muskets on our shoulders. I look to my left at Sophia, and see a warrior prepared for battle. She's focused straight ahead with her eyes moving side to side scanning the forest. Sophia senses that I am looking at her and she turns her head toward me. There are no words said.

Her eyes are telling me, "I love you. We'll get through this."

We both understand that these could be our last moments together. Sophia slides toward me, I'm preparing to receive a kiss good-bye. Then she punches me in the arm.

She smiles, and with a confident tone of voice she tells me, "We'll get through this Johann." As she is turning her head forward, she says, "Now let's kick some ass!"

Abraham walks out in front of us. He turns to face us and with sword in hand he addresses us all, "Steady now, remember, to hold your fire until the enemy is close enough to get a certain kill. Aim small. Squeeze the trigger, don't pull it. And remember, concentrate on the target. Don't rush your shot!"

The Indians begin talking, "Bilagaana ei faa laa woya hoi hahe!"

Then, from behind us, "Hahai oe oehaii ani!" We hear them continue talking from all around us.

Abraham calls to us as arrows are flying past him, "They're trying to get into your heads. Don't allow them to get to you."

After a few more minutes the Redskins stop. I don't know what is worse their talking, or the silence.

A Redskin stands up, front and center and cries-out, "Hahoia! Hahoia!"

I'm thinking, "That's Black Hawk."

He's standing tall with a red warrior's head roach made of porcupine guard hair on his head. He is a magnificent and dreadful leader, reminiscent of Baron Gutenriemer. The rest of the warriors now stand up and charge at us from all directions. There is about fifty of them running at us hollering at the top of their lungs.

Abraham orders. "Hold your fire men! Hold, wait until they get closer. Pick one target and aim at a small point in the center of his chest. Wait until the enemy is thirty steps out from you before you shoot! Hold your fire, hold it…hold it… OK, shoot!"

We all begin firing. Twenty warriors tumble forward dead and wounded, eliminating almost half of our opposition in one volley. Now the Redskins begin shooting their muskets and bows on the run back at us while on the run which affects their accuracy. Nonetheless, many of us are hit. After returning fire with muskets and arrows, the enemy grabs their war clubs and tomahawks and continue their advance on us.

Abraham directed each one of us to make an eight-foot lance. Which is laying on the ground by our side for just this very moment. Strapped to our side is a club or hatchet. Sophia and I raise our lances at the enemy impaling one of the charging Redskins. The battle has now elevated to hand-to-hand combat. The enemy has trained for this kind of fighting all of their lives.

I turn to look for Sophia and say, "Get behind me!"

Then I see her lunge past me. The tip of her lance pierces the chest of a warrior that is charging at my back. With Sophia's spear sticking out of his chest, the warrior grabs hold of her lance with both hands. He spins, wrenching the spear from her hands and runs at her. The butt end of the spear runs into the wagon that's located behind her, driving the lance deeper into his chest and preventing the warrior from reaching her. I then swing my hatchet at the Indian splitting his head open above his left eye.

Another warrior comes at me from my right side swinging his war club. I shield the blow with my musket that I'm holding in my left hand and swing my hatchet at him, hitting him deep in his forearm causing him to drop his club. The warrior immediately lunges at me, knocking me down on my back. He is on top of me, reaching for my hatchet. He leans his head down and bites my right arm, making me release the weapon. Then, suddenly, he drops limp on top of me. Exhausted, I struggle to roll the warrior off of me. When I crawl out from under him, I look up to see Sophia, there is blood splattered on her face and chest. She's leaning down and reaching to help me up.

The Redskins are running from the battlefield. We all are cheering, Hooray! Sie uber den feind! Hooray! The odds were against us, but we are victorious! Black Hawk and his warriors had not lost a battle until this point. We owe our victory to Abraham. He understood the enemy and he knew how to beat them.

"Where is he? We owe this victory to him! I must thank him for our success. Where is he?"

I look at Sophia. In silence, she points to the ground where Abraham directed our defense. He had died of a wound from a musket ball that struck him in his neck. My jubilance turns to sadness as I look at Abraham lying on his back expressionless. His eyes are wide open, staring at the treetops. I then turn around to see our dead and wounded comrades around me. They are surrounded by their grieving families.

We are victorious, but it came at a very high price. Seven men died in the battle; six others, including my good friend George, are wounded. Two of the men are suffering from wounds of which they probably won't survive. Two women and a twelve-year-old child were killed.

I watch Sophia stager over to a nearby wagon and sits down on the ground. She's staring straight ahead with a blank expression on her face. She begins shaking as she's trying to hold back her tears. In the time that I have known her and all that we have been through, I have never seen her show emotion before this time. I walk over to her and sit down next to her, put my arm around her and hold her tight while she is quietly crying.

As I'm holding Sophia, I'm thinking that we are still in danger of another attack. There isn't time for grieving. Black Hawk has never lost a battle. If I were in Black Hawk's moccasins, I would attack again and turn his defeat into a victory. His pride and the confidence that his warriors have in him are at stake. Turning this defeat into a victory would be important to his warrior's morale. I think, more importantly to Black Hawk, it is essential for his legacy! We don't have time to mourn our losses. It is critical that we get to the safety of Fort Dearborn before dark. I must find Solomon and George to help me get these people motivated to leave this place.

Solomon and George are natural leaders. It is amazing to watch them work. Together they are able to motivate the people, even in this sad time. They know what needs to be done and how to get people to accomplish it. George convinced the Poles of the urgency to get ready to leave for the safety of Fort Dearborn. In less than an hour we have our wounded and dead loaded in the wagons. The horses that we can find are hitched to the wagons. We are going to have to leave half of the wagons and most of the pull carts behind. Solomon asked one of the women to pick up the muskets, including the enemy's muskets that were left on the battlefield up and put them in one of the wagons.

We are pushing hard to get to the fort. No one wants to be on this trail after dark. Each man has his musket in hand. Most of us have one of the muskets that was picked up on the battlefield loaded and ready to shoot as well.

Illinois became the 21st state on December 3, 1818. In 1830 95 percent of the state's white population is confined to the southernmost 20 percent of the state. Native Americans were in control of the rest. The Potawatomi, Illinois, Ottawa, and Miami tribes ceded the northern part of the state to the United States Government in 1830.

The sun had set as we pull into the village of Chicago. Where is the booming community that George Walker told me about? This is a disappointment for Walker and his Polish settlers. But it is actually just the way that Solomon had described it.

As we approach the fort, I want to cheer with joy. But then, I think about my friends who died today defending our wagon train. I'm thinking of their family who is feeling such pain in their hearts. This day was exhausting, and we are all glad that it is over. It's a relief for us to be in the safety of Fort Dearborn.

We approach the gate where two guards step forward with their weapons across their chests. In a loud voice one of them orders, "Who goes there? State your business."

A Sergeant walks over to us. Solomon tells him who we are and of our battle with Black Hawk. The sergeant immediately orders Solomon and me to follow him to the General's quarters for debriefing. George tells the sergeant about our dead and wounded. The sergeant orders a detail to take the wounded to the hospital and take the dead to the morgue.

We follow the Sergeant on the quickstep into the fort and across the courtyard. We pass an American flag on a tall pole on our way to the General's quarters. It is located in the center of the fort. When we get to a door the Sergeant knocks loudly. A deep, commanding voice calls out, "Enter."

The Sergeant turns to us and orders, "Stay here."

He enters the office leaving the door partially open behind him. I have never seen an American general. I can't help myself. I peek around the door. There he is, a wide shouldered man sitting tall behind a desk with a writing quill in hand. He's wearing a clean and pressed blue uniform. There are polished brass buttons down the front and gold-colored emblems with stars on each of his shoulders.

FORT DEARBORN

The Sergeant orders us to enter the General's office and makes the introductions, "This is General Hull."

The Sergeant orders us to enter the General's office and makes the introductions, "This is General Hull."

The Sergeant turns to the General and says, "General Hull, these are the pilgrims who claim that they were involved in a skirmish with Black Hawk."

The General began his questioning with, "Where did this encounter take place?"

The General continued the debriefing in a very articulate manner asking about every detail of the battle. He ended our interrogation by saying, "Gentlemen, I was skeptical when the Sergeant told me that you survived a battle against Black Hawk. Your party is the first and only one, to defeat him in battle."

"Sergeant, take the wounded to the Surgeon's quarters. Show these gentlemen and their party to our mess hall and have the cooks prepare dinner for them. Make arrangements for the burial of our fallen heroes tomorrow, with full military honors."

The General stands up and dismisses the Sergeant. He walks around his desk, smiles and in a cordial tone of voice says, "Gentlemen dinner will take an hour to prepare. Would you join me in a glass of rye? I would like to hear more about your encounter with Black Hawk."

He points with open hand to a table and chairs and walks to his liquor cabinet pulls out a bottle and three glasses. As he's pouring the rye, the General says, "Please sit down. You may call me William. Now, please tell me of your friend Abraham."

The three of us talked about the battle and our trip across Indiana. We are drinking rye until there is a knock on the door and a soldier announces that dinner is ready.

After dinner, the sergeant that we had met earlier comes to our table and tells us that he has the honor to be our host while we are in Chicago. He says we were invited to stay at the fort as long as we like while our wounded are healing in the fort's hospital. When we leave the mess hall, the soldiers are in the courtyard, lined up at attention and saluting.

Sophia quietly says, "Look Johann, the flag is set at half-mast. What does that mean?"

William Hull was born June 24, 1753, in Derby, Conn. He joined a local militia 1775, at the outbreak of the American Revolutionary War. He rapidly rose in rank to lieutenant colonel.

*During the war of 1812, Hull earned the rank of Brigadier General in command of the Army of the Northwest. ***

Jhn Hull

We accepted the General's offer and stayed in Chicago for two weeks. Our wounded have had the time they needed to heal under the sergeant's care. And the grieving wives needed this time to be near their husband's grave sites.

George came to talk to Solomon and me this morning to say that the Poles have talked among themselves. Town of Chicago is not the boom town that the promoters led them to believe that it was. The Polish families have decided to go on to Milwaukee with us.

I say to George, "I'm delighted that you and the Poles are going to Milwaukee. I pledge to take care of the widows and their children in Milwaukee."

* Wikipedia

I can't wait to tell Sophia the good news!

We talked to the others in our group, and it's decided that we will leave for Milwaukee tomorrow morning. Solomon, George, and I go to call on General Hull to tell him of our plans to leave in the morning and to thank him for his hospitality. The General informs us that it will take three days to get to Milwaukee.

He continues, "Outside the gate, you will find the Green Bay Trail. Go north on that trail and it will take you to the Town of Milwaukee."

He alerts us that he received a report that Black Hawk had attacked Fort Atkinson in the Wisconsin Territory five days ago. Fort Atkinson is about fifty miles west of the Green Bay Trail.

The General goes on to say, "The Green Bay Trail, like the Great Lakes Trail is a narrow passageway cut through the wilderness. You won't find any bridges but I'm confident that your people are accustomed to forging rivers. I'm sorry, but I won't be able to provide an escort for you. I simply don't have the troops available for that right now."

We are spending the day preparing for our departure in the morning. When that task is completed Sophia and I go around to the townspeople and soldiers that we had met to let them know that we are leaving in the morning and to say goodbye.

I go to the General Store/Post Office to get some items that we need for our trip to Milwaukee. Sophia wrote a letter to Anna for me, so I'll mail it while I'm at the Post Office. Among the wanted posters is a picture of Sophia! There is a $10,000 reward for information leading to her safe return of her! What the Hell is this all about? Well, I know that it's Baron von Gutenriemer. What would make him think that Sophia could be in Chicago?

I tear the poster off of the wall, walk to the fort, and into the General's office. "General Hull, I need to talk to you about this."

The General interrupts me and responds as he opens his desk drawer and pulls out the poster, "I know what you are here for. There is a man looking for Sophia. He was here ten minutes ago. I ordered some men to go out find you and Sophia."

He slams the poster down on his desk. In a loud voice, he demands, "I want some damn answers! What the Hell is this all about?"

I reply, "I can explain everything you want to know General. But first we must find Sophia. She is in great danger!"

The General responds, "Okay, I'll order some more men to look for her. You can go. We will finish this conversation later. Look out for the man that's wearing green coat and orange knickers. He works for Baron Gutenriemer. Check back with me in an hour."

I thank the General for his help and leave his office. I'm frantically looking everywhere that I think Sophia would be and asking everyone that I see if they have seen her. Several of the people that I have talked to are saying that the man with a strong German accent was showing the poster around and asking about Sophia. They all said that they didn't give him any information.

I'm thinking, it's just a matter of time until someone gives the Baron's agent information on how to find Sophia. I don't know for certain that the agent has not already found her already. The ten-thousand-dollar reward would make any man in this town wealthy beyond his wildest dreams. It's just too much money for some people to pass up. Even my good friends may be rethinking the statement that they gave to the Baron's agent. The soldiers who are looking for her may even turn her in for the reward. That kind of money is more than fifty times their annual income.

I've looked everywhere in this little town. I think to myself, "What have I missed?"

Wait! I realize that I have talked to everyone in town except George and Solomon. If I can find them, maybe I'll find Sophia with them. Where would they be? I go to the wagon where George is keeping his few possessions in. His wagon is empty. Solomon is missing too. They're probably together. Now, where are they?

Where is the best place to hide in this little town of forty houses? You can't hide for long here so one has to get out of here. The best place to hide Sophia is in Milwaukee. I'm hoping that Solomon and George are with her. I think that they are going to Milwaukee! I go to the stable and buy a horse and saddle. I stop to get my musket and I'm on my way.

Sophia can't be much more than a few hours ahead of me. As soon as I turn the first bend in the trail, I see the yellow ribbon hanging from a tree that Sophia likes to wear in her hair. I am so relieved to know that Sophia was here. I'm trotting to catch up to her. I wasn't told my horse's name. I'll call her Bootsie. After three hours of trotting to catch Sophia, I can see her!

As I spur Bootsie, I call out to her, "Sophia! Sophia!" She pulls on the reins, turns around and spurs her horse. Her horse is at a full run. When she gets to me, she jumps of her horse and pulls me off of mine. She knocks me off balance onto my back. We embrace each other laughing and crying for joy.

She says to me. "I'm so sorry that I left you behind. Please forgive me. I was afraid that you wouldn't be able to find me."

"There is no need to apologize. You did the right thing by leaving Chicago. You would be in your father's custody right now if you would not have fled. I am so happy that you are safe."

I look up to see George and Solomon standing over us. Solomon is trying to hold back a smile as he bends down, extends his hand to me and helps me up to my feet. George crouches down grabs Sophia around her waist and lifts her up and sets her on her feet. I put my arms around Solomon and I give him a hug to show my gratitude. Then I do the same to George. I look them both in the eyes and say with sincere appreciation, "Thank you both for saving my Sophia from going back to a life of bondage. I'll never be able to repay you both for what you have done for us."

After a humbling moment, Solomon points up the trail and responds, "Wisconsin is that way. Let's get moving. Nous brulons la lumiere du jour." (We're burning daylight.)

We all mount our horses and begin trotting up the trail. Sophia and I are riding next to each other. George and Solomon are about thirty feet ahead of us, to give us some space. They are talking to each other in low voices, planning the next move. They agree that a $10,000 reward for turning in Sophia is going to get someone to talk. Someone in Chicago may have told the Baron's agent the Sophia was in Chicago already. We don't know that the Baron's agents aren't following us right now! We can assume that it's just a matter of time until we must confront the Baron's agents.

It's getting dark. Solomon, who has traveled this trail many times, tells us that we are near a Potawatomi village called Waukegan. The Potawatomi people living there had been peaceful in the past. But with Chief Tecumseh's resistance movement against white settlers, things may have changed since Solomon was here last. Solomon suggests that we go off of the trail about one hundred paces to setup camp. As a precaution we won't have a fire tonight.

As we are setting up camp, Sophia proclaims to us, "I'm putting the three of you in danger and I won't allow it anymore. I appreciate everything the three of you are doing for me and I love you all for it, but I've decided that I'm going to turn myself into my father. I am going back to Chicago in the morning, and I want the three of you to go on to Milwaukee. Better yet, I insist that the three of you turn me in and split the reward. Don't try to talk me out of this. I have thought about it all afternoon and it is my final decision."

We aren't expecting to hear that, and we're all caught off, guard. I immediately respond with an emotional plea, "You can't do that. I won't let you!"I pause while I try to think of something

143

that will convince her to change her mind. I'm thinking that I need to come up with something quick before she responds to my stupid plea. I know, I'll try this, "You aren't a burden. I'm thinking, that's a good opening line. Now how do I follow-up. Oh I have it. I reach out to her with both hands and hold onto her hands.

I look into her eyes and say, "I need you with me, Sophia. My dream of a life in Wisconsin has you in it, right next to me. I knew from the moment that I first saw you that I needed you in my life. Remember that evening on the porch at the hotel?"

We talked about our new life with each other, "At that moment I realized that I would spend my life with you. We both understood that we came from different worlds and knew that we are going to confront obstacles every day. This is just an obstacle, and we will overcome it together."

Sophia is looking at me without saying a word. She lets go of my hands and turns, away from me then walks to her bedroll, and sits down.

Solomon leans in toward George and whispers, "Well done. If that didn't convince her we'll have to tie her up, gag her, blindfold her, and carry her to Milwaukee."

It's early in the evening but Sophia doesn't want to talk so we just lay down and fall asleep.

Chapter Eleven

Wisconsin!

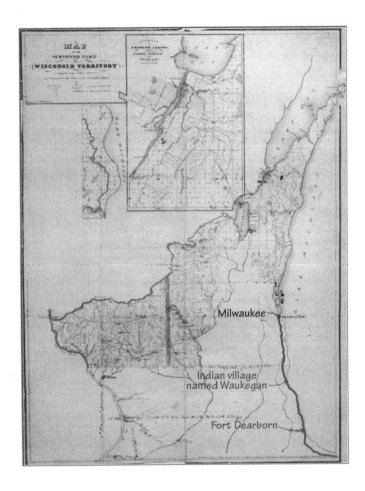

The four of us have been riding for three hours this morning. We have now crossed the Wisconsin Territory mile marker. We have reached Wisconsin! Sophia is with us too, and no, she's not gagged, blindfolded, and tied up.

It's painful to me when I think of how the Baron is still trying to control his daughter's life. Sophia is nothing more than a possession to him. We had traveled more than four thousand miles to get away from Sophia's father and the son-of-a-bitch found us! A reason that Sophia chose the Wisconsin wilderness to hide from her father because it's on the western edge of civilization. I feel like we are right back to where we were when we left Mecklenburg. Sophia is trying to be strong but every time she thinks about him, she quivers with fear. We don't talk about it, but we both know that the Baron has found my darling Sophia, and it's a matter of time until I must confront him. How do I protect her against a man that is as powerful as the Baron?

Tonight, we will camp near a place the Potawatomi call "Nodek bgednek tot bgednat." (Windy point on the lake) English-speaking trappers call it "Wind Point." Like last night, we will camp one hundred paces off the trail again and we won't have a fire.

It's a sunny morning our goal is to reach Milwaukee, by the end of the day. Solomon has a house in Milwaukee, and he has offered his house as a place for us to stay until we find a permanent place to live.

It's a sunny morning. We started riding up the trail about an hour ago. Solomon announces that we are getting close to Milwaukee. It has been such a long, hard journey from Mecklenburg. Now, we are almost at our destination.

None of us has talked all morning. George is probably thinking about his Polish friends that he left in Chicago. And, Sophia, is worrying about how she is going to evade her father's agents. Knowing her, she is worrying that I am going to try to confront her father.

As we're riding up the trail and I'm thinking of my mother and father. How I miss them. If only they could be with Sophia and me at our new home in Milwaukee. I had no idea how difficult this journey was going to be. I don't know if Mother could have made it through Indian country. And Father, he would be proud of how I stepped up and became the man that I have become. Mutter, Vater, I think about you both every day.

I'm thinking of my sister and best friend, Anna. I'm so worried about her. We haven't heard from her since we were in Harrisburg. Although how would she contact us. I pray that the Captain is treating her well. She had never in her life, been on her own and away from our family. If the Captain hurts Anna, I will kill him! As soon as I get to Milwaukee, I think that I will ask Sophia to write her a letter for me and to let her know that I arrived safely. I'll give Anna Solomon's address so that she can write to me. My brothers, Dietrich and Otto were on their way to fight Indians when I saw them last. Just like every time they leave, I'm afraid that I may never see them again. I told them that I was going to be in Milwaukee, so I won't be surprised if they came knocking on my door someday.

Oh, that's just wishful thinking.

There is a fork in the trail and Solomon takes the right branch called Indian Trail. Solomon says, "We're getting close to Milwaukee."

I see a cabin across the swamp on our left. Solomon says, "That's Doc Chase's home. Through the woods on the right is Joel Wilcox's farm. He has two squaws for wives."

Solomon continues, "This house is where Alex Stuart lives. I'll introduce you to him soon."

Chapter Twelve

Milwaukee!

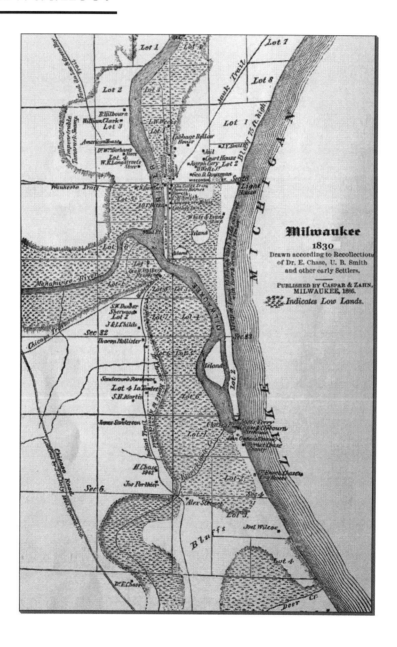

We are approaching a toll bridge at a river that Solomon is calling the Kinnikinic River. I give a penny to the owner of the bridge and he raises the gate. We continue north. Solomon points out the home of Josh Portlier a French fur trader. There is a farm up the trail on the left side owned by a Swede named, Jakob Sanderson who is a carpenter by trade. Jakob also owns the tavern on our right. I'm sure I'll meet Jakob soon. A quarter of a mile past Jacob's house we pass three farms. Solomon tells us that they are owned by Yankees. Their names are Hollester, Childs, and Sherwood.

We are riding on high ground that has large swamps on both sides of the trail. The swamps are loaded with wild rice and game birds of all species. The sound of ducks, geese, and cranes is deafening. We're now riding parallel to the Milwaukee River. As we approach the point where the Menominee River flows into the Milwaukee River. George stops. Sophia, Solomon, and I stop and turn around to see George stopped and scanning the area and looking down over the fifty foot drop on both sides of him into the swamps. George dismounts looks down, and kicks off the leaves to expose rich black soil. He stands in silence for a minute looking from side to side.

Then he speaks, "Gentlemen, Milady, this highpoint is going to be my home. I'm going to build my house near those five oak trees." (George points north).

> *George Walker was able to purchase the land from an Irishman named Dunbar Sherwood. He built his house with windows overlooking the swamps as he prophesied it the day we first came to Milwaukee. He later developed the land around his house into residential and commercial properties. Townspeople began calling the neighborhood "Walker's Point".*

Town of Milwaukee

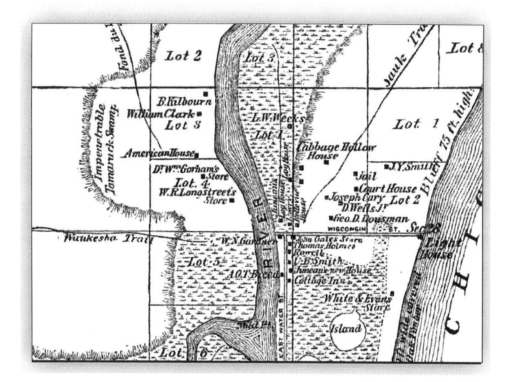

We wait patiently until George is finished dreaming about his future home, then we ride down the hill to a ferry. We board it and cross the Milwaukee River. On the East side of the river, I am pleased to find that there is a general store, a hotel, several saloons, and houses. We have arrived in the Village of Milwaukee!

We follow Solomon as he leads us north on Water Street to Jauk Trail. We turn North on Jauk Trail for one quarter mile to Solomon's home. It's a beautiful house with his trading post on the first floor. Solomon shows us to our rooms and after we settle in, he offers to buy us dinner at the Cabbage Hollow House Hotel. After dinner we order a round of ale and toast to Milwaukee, and then we toast to our friendship.

We wake up early. It's our first day in Milwaukee. I get up before sunrise. At first light, I take a walk in my new hometown. I'm drawn to the Lake Michigan bluff. Standing at the edge, I look down to see a beach that is 90 feet below me. The sun is just beginning to peak over the lake. I've never seen anything quite so magnificent!

I wipe the dew off a tree stump and sit down to watch seagulls soaring effortlessly along the bluff. I hear them calling, "ha, ha, ha, ha."

The waves are lapping gently on the beach below. Occasionally, flocks of ducks fly by low over the water. There is an orange glow forming on the horizon. The glow is slowly, almost imperceptibly getting brighter. Now I see a sliver of brilliant orange peaking over the horizon, promising a new day. I need to find a way to live in a place where I can experience these wonders every morning for the rest of my life. After sitting on this stump until the sun is up, I walk back to Solomon's house. Sophia is sweeping the front porch. Solomon is at work in his trading post. And George, I'm told that he is out asking around to locate the owner of the land that he was admiring yesterday on the other side of the river.

There is a sign over Solomon's trading post door. I ask, "What does the sign say, Sophia?"

She answers, "The American Fur Company."

I tell Sophia, "If Solomon needs me, tell him I'm taking a walk down the street to acquaint myself with our new hometown. I'll also try to find a room for us to rent."

Solomon's house is on the north end of town. I'm walking south on Jauk Trail. It's a wide, dirt road. There is a little stone building with bars on the windows and door. I assume that it is the jail. Next to the jail is a small one-story log building with a tall man standing on the porch.

I walk over to him. "Hello, I'm Johann Kemp. I just arrived in town late yesterday. I'm staying with Solomon Juneau and his wife Josette temporarily."

The man on the porch replies, "It's nice to meet you, Mr. Kemp. My name is Jamie Smith. Folks around here call me JT."

He goes on to tell me that he manages the Firean House saloon and hotel for widow Firean.

I tell JT, "My wife and I are looking for a place to live. Do you have any vacancies?"

He replies, "I have two rooms available. Would you and your wife like to see them?"

I answer, "Yes, I would. Are you available to show it now? I know where it is. I'll get my wife and meet you at the hotel in an hour."

Sophia and I did rent a room at the Firean's House Hotel. It has an upper deck out front. I'm looking forward to spending evenings with Sophia out on the deck. We are going to move in this afternoon after I talk to Solomon and let him know our plans.

When I meet with Solomon and tell him that I will be moving into the Firean House Hotel tonight, he asks me to start working for him tomorrow morning. This will be my first time working for anyone besides my father. I'm looking forward to it.

For the remainder of the day, Sophia and I are spending our time meeting our new neighbors. There are about 100 people of European heritage living in Milwaukee and the surrounding area. They are mostly Yankees. The rest are first and second-generation Americans of English, French and Irish nationalities. There are also many Indians. They are living along the Milwaukee, Kinnik,inic and Menominee rivers and the surrounding marshlands. The Indians are mainly Potawatomi but there are also, Indians of the Menominee, Ojibwa, and, Ho-Chunck tribes. Solomon tells me that the Indians are peaceful and pleasant neighbors that stay to themselves.

In the winter representatives from each tribe will bring their small animal pelts to Solomon or Josh Porthier to trade. I've been working for Solomon all week. Today is Sunday and I have the day off. Sophia and I take the ferry to the west side of the Milwaukee River. I can see that there is a new dirt road being made. Along the road are a few houses that are being built. Because I was in the trade, I couldn't resist walking up to the carpenters and talking to them. They are Irish so Sophia is our interpreter.

The Irishmen were a pleasant sort. They had just arrived in Milwaukee last week, so we had several things in common. They say that when the owner of this development heard that they are carpenters he hired all three of them on the spot. It is interesting talking to these carpenters about their tools and building techniques.

Sophia has absolutely no interest in our carpenter topic. So, when she sees an opportunity, she jumps in and asks the men how long they had been in America. The Irishmen tells Sophia that they had arrived in Baltimore just two weeks before we did. They went on to say that the three of them were partners in Dublin, Ireland. Hard times have fallen upon Ireland and there wasn't much work for carpenters.

A well-dressed gentleman walks up to us, and the carpenters quickly get back to work.

He introduces himself to us. "Hello, I'm Byron Kilbourn. Welcome to

Kilbourn Town. Can I help you? Are you in the market for a new house?"

Byron Kilbourn
B 9/8/1801 D 12/16/1870

"No sir, we are staying at the hotel." I answer.

Kilbourn asks, "I'm building a general store. Do you have experience managing a store? I'm also building a new hotel and saloon and I'm looking for a manager. Are you a brewer, a tinner, or a carpenter?"

I answer, "I am a carpenter I'd like to help you sir, but I have a job with Solomon Juneau on the other side of the river in Juneau Town."

I'm interrupted, "You don't want to work for that no-good crook! He'll rob you blind!" What's he paying you? I'll pay you more. When do you want to start? Tomorrow?"

"I'm honored by your offer sir. I'm sorry Mr. Kilbourn. I've made a commitment. I'm going to be working for Mr. Juneau."

Kilbourn argues, "You're making a stupid mistake. I'm going to crush Juneau and when I do, you won't have a job! I won't give you another chance. Think about my offer, and I'll talk to you tomorrow. Now get out of my town!"

I turn to Sophia and say, "I have nothing more to say to this man, Sophia. Let's get out of here. Good day Mr. Kilbourn."

We turn and walk to the ferry. When we get out of hearing distance, I tell Sophia, "I wouldn't work for that man, even if he had the only job in Wisconsin."

Sophia replies, "I wouldn't allow you to work for him."

On our way back to our new home I ask Sophia; "Would you teach me how to write this evening?"

On our way back to our new home I ask Sophia; "Would you teach me how to write this evening?"

"Of course, I will Johann. But first I'll teach you how to read. You're a slow learner so, it may take more than just one evening." She responds kiddingly.

Sophia continues, "I have a better idea, after dinner, why don't you go down to the bar and get us each a pint of beer. Then you and I could go out on the hotel deck and celebrate our new home. We can begin your reading lessons tomorrow night. Okay?"

We find a bench behind the hotel and with JT's permission. I bring it up to the front balcony. After the sun went down, I got a jug of ale at the hotel bar and Sophia joins me on the front balcony. We toast to our new home at the Firean's House. This is our first permanent home we have ever had together.

"Sophia, I promise you that someday we will have our own house on our own farm. That is our dream." Sophia holds up her mug and says, "To our first home in Wisconsin!"

I take a long deep breath, and slowly exhale. This is the first time that I feel that I can relax in months. It's just momentary, but for now I feel at peace.

Next thing I know Sophia is shaking me. I hear, "Wake-up, Johann. Wake-up. We need to go inside." I awake to see that I'm on the balcony. I must have fallen asleep.

It's my first day grading fur with Solomon. I'm looking forward to getting started. Solomon tells me that I will be shadowing him until I learn the business. I'm learning how to buy, grade and sort furs. Solomon told me that he expects that I will someday be good enough that he can promote me to a branch manager. I would then run one of the remote trading posts.

Meanwhile, as I might have guessed, Sophia isn't sitting idly in the hotel room. She has been out meeting and charming the townspeople all day. She met the owner of the hotel, Mrs. Firean. They talked most of the afternoon and struck up quite a friendship. In addition to the hotel, Mrs. Firean owns the gristmill, a sawmill, and a brewery.

Among other things Mrs. Firean talked about her business. Since her husband died last year, Mrs. Firean has been trying to find a man to be an accountant for her businesses. There just isn't a man in Milwaukee with the education to balance a set of books.

Sophia responds, "My father had my mentors train me in accounting. I have been running the books for some of my father's businesses. If you like, I would be happy to help you out for a while. I'm sure I can get things back on track for you."

Mrs. Firean sat straight up. Her eyes wide open with excitement over Sophia's offer. "When can you start? How much do you need to be paid? Please help me? I will provide an office for you at my home if you like. Please say you will. If you can do what you say you can, I'll provide a house for you and your husband to live in."

Sophia responds to Mrs. Firean, "I'll talk to Johann when he gets home from work tonight. I'll let you know what we decide tomorrow morning."

I'm anxious to tell Sophia about my first day at work when I get home. The moment I walk in the door Sophia begins telling me about her new job.

I stand straight and tell her, "I won't allow it! How would it look having my women working in what is a man's field!"

Oops, big mistake.

After a twenty-minute lecture, I do fold and agree that going to work for Mrs. Firean is a good idea.

Sophia arrived at Mrs. Firean's home at 7:00 AM and negotiated a compensation package that included Mrs. Firean providing a house for Sophia and me to live in. Sophia began working for Mrs. Firean at 8:00 AM.

With Sophia's energy and natural management skills Mrs. Firean's businesses are beginning to flourish. Mrs. Firean is now opening a general store and a drug store on Water Street. Under Sophia's direction Mrs. Firean is investing her profits into buying up properties on Water Street and Wisconsin Street.

Meanwhile, George Walker is developing Walker's Point. The group of Poles that traveled with us to Fort Dearborn decides to move to Milwaukee. They all settled in Walker's Point. It's now our Polish community. George is a brilliant promoter. He is advertising in Polish speaking newspapers in New York, Boston, and Baltimore, promoting Walkers Point. His campaign is successful and is drawing Poles into his development.

George's success is of course getting the attention of Juneau and Kilbourn. Their real estate developments are having only modest success this year.

Solomon asks me, "What is George's secret?"

"Why don't we just go over to him and ask?" I respond.

And we do. It's good to see George. We have all been so busy that the three of us haven't gotten together since we arrived in Milwaukee. That was six months ago! George invites us to go over to his new saloon and have a beer with him. The three of us spend the whole afternoon telling stories, drinking, and laughing.

I'm looking at my friends and thinking, "I've never had better friends than these two guys." I hold up my mug and we toast to our friendship.

I look out the window and it's dark outside. "Well, my friends it's getting late. I think that we've been here for at least four hours. George, you are living the life of a bachelor, but I'm not and I think it's time for me to go home. So long my friends."

Solomon realizes that it's 7:45 and the ferry stops running at 8:00 so he finishes his beer and we hurry on our way.

We had so much fun at our little reunion that we forgot to talk to George about what we went there for. Solomon went back across the river later in the week to talk business. George showed him how to identify his target market and find the newspapers in his target cities.

Ads have been running in German-speaking newspapers and we were beginning to reap the rewards. German-speaking people are now arriving in large numbers. Solomon tells me that I'll be working in his real estate development business until November when the fur business picks-up.

The seasons are changing, and we will experience our first winter in Wisconsin. Immigration has stopped in our little community for the winter season. Hopefully it will resume in spring. Solomon and I are busy at the fur trading business, and we expect to stay busy through the winter, as the furs are prime in the cold temperatures and demand higher prices. Business has slowed for the winter season for Sophia and Mrs. Firean, so Sophia has more time to spend around our house.

Massacre at Bad Axe August 1-2, 1832

General Atkinson's federal troops pursued Black Hawk's Fox and Sauk followers for more than 200 miles across northern Illinois and southern Wisconsin.

After holding off Atkinson at the battle of Wisconsin Heights. (Located 1.5 miles south of Sauk City) Black Hawk led his followers toward the Mississippi River. Black Hawk's followers were reduced to 400 starving men, women, and children when they reached the Mississippi at the mouth of the bad Axe River in Wisconsin Territory. Upon reaching the river, they began building rafts and canoes to make the quarter mile crossing of the Mississippi River.

On August first, under a white flag, Black Hawk attempted to surrender to US troops. Fearing that it was a trick, US soldiers fired upon him, killing twenty five warriors.

*1300 US troops and Wisconsin militia arrived in the night and attacked in the morning, indiscriminately killing men, women, and children. Those that attempted to cross the river were killed from a steamboat with canon and musket fire. The few that reached the west shore were hunted down and killed by Sioux warriors acting at the request of the US Army. ***

* Wisconsin Historical Society

It's now springtime. Winter was long for Sophia, but it is the busy time in the fur business. I've been looking forward to spring when things slow down for me, and it's finally arrived.

For the first time since December, I'm finding time to go sit on my favorite stump overlooking Lake Michigan. The ducks are returning in flocks so large that they block out the rising sun as they fly north.

The sun is now up. I had better get home before Sophia leaves for work. On the way home, I see Jacob Sullivan and his son Abe. They are plowing their field. It brings back memories of my grandfather and I working the Baron's fields. I miss the smell of freshly plowed soil. Farming is in my blood and I miss it. I've been so busy over this last year that I haven't had time to think about it much until now. It's still my dream to have my own land and work my own farm. I'm afraid that Sophia won't want to move away from her friends and job when we are able to afford to buy land. On my way home I notice a new face in town. I haven't seen anyone new since last Fall. So of course, need to meet this guy. He's well dressed. That in itself is very odd in Milwaukee.

"Hello, my name is Johann Kemp. You're new in Milwaukee. Welcome to our town."

The stranger replies, "I'm Daniel Wells. I just arrived in town last night. I came in from the state of Maine."

We talk for a while. He seems to be a pleasant fellow. Very smart and well educated. "Daniel, tell me if you would, where is Maine?" I ask in my broken English.

Daniel replies in German, "Maine is the

Daniel Wells Jr.

161

state in the Northeast corner of our country." He continues, "Forgive me for being assumptive but my wife immigrated from Hamburg, so I understand that it takes some time to learn about our vast country."

I'm thinking to myself, "This man can put words together better than anyone I've ever listened to. He's using words that I have never heard before. He can make me feel stupid without being insulted. This guy should be in politics."

Then I say, "What brought you to Milwaukee?"

"Well, I was reading an editorial in a Polish speaking newspaper out of Boston. It was written by a man named Walker. His article convinced me of the many opportunities in Milwaukee. My mercantile business in Maine was struggling so I closed shop and moved here. I must say, it's not the boomtown that Mr. Walker portrayed it to be. Do you know this, Walker? I would like to have a conversation with him."

Daniel Wells Jr. b.1808 d 1902

Wells engaged in banking, lumbering, land speculating and land developing in Milwaukee county.

Politics: Served as probate judge in Milwaukee.
        Member of Wisc. Territorial Council 1838-1840
        Elected to, 33rd & 34th Congress representing
        Wisconsin's first district.

At the time of his death Wells was the wealthiest person in Wisconsin.

*Buried: Forest Home Cemetery, Milwaukee ***

Millicent (Millie) Wells

* Wisconsin Historical Society

I don't want to tell Daniel where to find George. At least not until Daniel is in a better frame of mind. Given time, I think he will see the opportunities that Milwaukee must offer.

I spend the afternoon with Daniel showing him around our little town and introducing him to everyone we met. I can sense that as he sees our little town and meets our wonderful residents I'm avoiding the not so wonderful ones. I think that Daniel is beginning to like it here. He is seeing how he could fit in and what he can offer. At the end of the day, I invite Daniel and his wife, Millie to join Sophia and me for dinner.

Millie and Sophia become instant friends. They have so much in common, as Millie was also born into wealth. Millie's maiden name was Millicent Voght, daughter of Baron Casper von Voght of Hamburg. Sophia and Millie have not found anyone in America that they really can relate to until now. They are acting like the sisters that they never had. Daniel sees it too.

I think that Millie's happiness living here is the reason that will convince him to stay in Milwaukee.

Millie tells Sophia and I that her father, Baron Von Voght is an extremely successful merchant and social reformer in Hamburg. His radical reformation ideas of social change and peasant rights have made enemies of many noblemen and landowners in the German-speaking kingdoms. Baron von Gutenriemer being one of them. Sophia's father blames Baron von Voght and his like thinking noblemen for his financial losses.

The evening with Daniel and Millie seemed to fly by. The four of us truly enjoy each other's company.

Unlike Sophia, Millie adores her father and corresponds with him frequently. The Millie's father has come to America to visit Millie occasionally. He is enthusiastic about investing in

America. During one of his trips, he financed a partnership with Daniel in his mercantile business.

Daniel has talked to Solomon and me openly about the process of purchasing land from the federal government for logging.

President Jackson has appointed General Henry Dodge as Wisconsin's first territorial governor. He will be sworn in on October 25th.

Solomon tells us, "I Met General Dodge last year when I had provided Chippewa Indian guides for him when he was chasing Black Hawk. He owes me a favor. I assure you that he will be looking for a cash contribution to his campaign fund before he will hear your request to buy federal land. Buying land in the frontier country requires political influence and political influence must be bought. With your contribution, he will most likely approve your request to buy land."

Solomon went on to say, "Gentlemen, I don't have any interest in the logging business. I do have interest in the shipping business. If you cut the lumber, I will ship it to eastern markets. I have been learning about ship building over the years. I have hired a master shipbuilder and I'm in the process of building a shipyard in Manitowoc. We will begin building shallow draft schooner ships for Great Lakes shipping within six months."

Solomon continues, "So you see, I'm way ahead of both of you on this. I've been waiting for Wisconsin to reach a population of 10,000 so that Wisconsin can be issued statehood. Lead was discovered in the Southeastern part of our Territory. Thousands of prospectors have been waiting for the Black Hawk war to end so that they could begin mining. Black Hawk's surrender now makes it safe for the miners to come to our territory, and they are coming by the thousands. We now are well over the population requirement for our people to petition for approval for statehood.

Surveyors have been working for years in southeastern Wisconsin. in anticipation of this moment and they are now finishing their work. The one key item that is missing at this point is, Dose Millie's father have interest in providing the funds to payoff the governor and buy the land from the federal government. The Government Land Office is in the town of Mineral Point. Mineral Point located in the southwestern part of Wisconsin. It takes five days to get there. If Baron von Voght is on board, you could be logging trees this coming summer."

Solomon Juneau *
Born: August 9, 1793,
Married: Josette Vieau
Died: November 14, 1856

Solomon Juneau   Josette Vieau Juneau

* Wisconsin Historical Society

Daniel and Millie chose to go forward and pursue the logging business. Millie wrote to her father and explained the venture the following day. Letters take eight to sixteen weeks to get to Hamburg. We will await the Baron's reply. It may take six months to receive an answer from him.

Meanwhile, Sophia and Mrs. Firean keep growing their businesses. They doubled the size of the Firean's House Hotel, and with the help of Solomon, they received a permit from the territorial government to build a dam on the Kinnikinic River. The dam should be completed by the end of the summer. New grist and sawmills are being built at the dam site.

Sophia is working long hours, six days a week. She has placed competent managers at each of Mrs. Firean's businesses and with some exceptions, they are all running smoothly and are profitable. Mrs. Firean understands that Sophia is the brains and energy of the companies. This morning, Mrs. Firean is waiting in Sophia's office when she returned from making a deposit at the bank.

Mrs. Firean said, "Sophia, I want to get right to the point. I am going to give you a full partnership in my businesses. You have earned it. You have built my businesses into what they are and I want to keep you happy. One other thing, I want you and Johann to call me Adela for now on."

Millie received her Tiffany's Blue Book *catalog and asked Sophia to get together for lunch today. Those two girls had so much fun going through the catalog page by page. They joked and laughed and drank beer for an hour. By the time lunch was served, they had filled in an entire order form and only stopped when they ran out of space on the order form. But they weren't done yet.

* Tiffany's department store in New York City produced America's first mail order catalog.

Millie says, "Sophia, we need to build ourselves new homes."

Sophia adds, "Right next to each other overlooking Lake Michigan."

Millie agrees and laughs out loud. Then, they stop laughing, they look at each other straight faced and say in a sober tone of voice, "We're serious aren't we."

Milwaukee is a very conservative community. The citizens in our little town just don't have the money to buy the kind of things that are in the Tiffany's catalog. When two women are filling out order forms for Tiffany's Blue Book in a restaurant, people notice, and it becomes the talk of the town. And then, the story is told it becomes exaggerated every time it's repeated. I overhear JT's wife, Anita talking about Sophia's shopping spree at the stables this afternoon and I'm angry!

It's been a long afternoon for me. All I can think about is Sophia's shopping spree. What is she thinking? I thought that we talked to each other before we spend money!

As I'm walking home at the end of the day, I'm thinking about what I'll say. Until today I've never even heard of such a thing as a catalog. It's a crazy idea. Who would ever order things from a company that is hundreds of miles away and have the products delivered to their home. It's a crazy idea! It'll never catch on.

I'm practicing what I'll say to her when I get home, "What were you thinking? There are so many more important things that we need, like a horse and buggy. And a barn to keep them in."

I walk up the porch steps and across the porch with heavy steps so that Sophia can hear me coming. Then I put on my angry face and swing the front door open. And, there is Sophia, standing at the door, glassy eyed with a tear forming in her left eye. Her voice is shaking, "I have something to tell you Johann. I am so sorry, but I had lunch with Millie, and I ordered some things from a mail order company. I interrupt her with a kiss on her mouth.

Then I look her in the eyes, "Don't explain. It's all right. I'm not mad at you. You have been working so hard this year. I want you to have those things from Tiffany's"

She jerks back a bit, her eyes open wide then she lowers her eyebrows and in a scolding tone of voice questions, "How did you know it was Tiffany's? I didn't say anything about Tiffany's! Where did you hear about Tiffany's?"

Caught off guard, I'm thinking, "What just happened here? How did I become the bad guy and the one in trouble?"

Now, I must explain myself. How does she do this? I had all the momentum just a moment ago. "Well dear, what's for dinner tonight?"

Sophia takes a step back and holds onto both of my hands. Her eyes are still damp with tears, and they are smiling widely. "Johann, I have some good news for you, Adela approached me this morning and offered me half ownership in her businesses. I told her that I would talk to you about it and get back to her in the morning."

I pause for a moment while I'm processing the news. "What is she asking for it?"

"Nothing. She just wants to make sure that I stay on with the company. She said that it is to show her appreciation for bringing her business from the brink of closing, into a very profitable enterprise."

Chapter Thirteen

Brass Ring

Sophia goes on to say, "Now that my income had more than doubled, do you think that we could afford to build our own house? We could talk to Jacob Sullivan and find out if he would sell us a lot on the back of his farm. I'm thinking about the place that you like to go to sit on that stump and watch the sun rise. Could we talk about it?"

I'm thinking, "Sophia knows that I have wanted to live on that spot since the first day that I arrived here. How could I say no?"

I reply, "Well, let's start saving our money. I will talk to Jacob next week and see what he would take for the land."

Sophia asks, "Would you ask him if he would sell two lots? Daniel and Millie will live next door."

"So, you and Millie were talking about this already, right? Does Daniel know about this too?"

Sophia answers with a sheepish smile, "I think they're talking about it right now."

"Okay, you have my approval but, I want to build our new home with my wife."

I fall to one knee. "Sophia, would you marry me?"

Sophia pauses, expressionless staring right through me without answering. Seconds pass that seems like forever, still no answer. I have a feeling in my stomach that I haven't felt since Anna left me. I'm thinking, "Say yes, say something, talk to me." Still staring straight ahead, silently, I see a tear slowly forming in her left eye, and then the right eye. Her lower lip is rising, and her chin begins to quiver. Her tear-soaked eyes turn to mine and her eyebrows are rising slightly. "Yes, I will, you fool."

She puts her arms around my neck and hugs me. I feel her tear-soaked cheek against mine. She begins sobbing for a moment and then, pulls back to look at me.

"I've been hoping that you would want to marry me since the day I saw you working in my father's stable. I was beginning to think you would never ask. Why did you keep me waiting so long?"

Lowering her eyebrows, she punches me in the arm. "Ouch!" Really hard this time! She means it.

She hugs me tight around my neck again and with her cheek on mine, she says in my ear, "I promise that I will be a good wife to you."

I quietly answer, "I know you will, and I'll be a good husband, I promise."

I take one step back and reach into my pocket and pull out a brass ring that I had Millie order for me from her Tiffany catalog. Reaching for her left hand, I tell my fiancé that, I would be so proud to have you wear this ring for the rest of our lives. I then slip it on her finger. A tear is forming in her left eye while a smile of joy is on her face. Staring down at the ring on her finger she turns her wrist slightly from side to side.

A smile is forming on her face. "I can't wait to show Millie in the morning!"

"When can we set the date, Johann? Have you thought about that? I want to get married soon. I want a church wedding and

I want to invite the whole town. I can't wait to let Anna know. She'll be so excited. I'll sit down and write to her tonight. I hope she can be here for our wedding. I've dreamed of being married in a church, but we don't have one in Milwaukee. What are we going to do about a church?"

I answer, "I've been thinking about it for a while now. The closest church was in the hamlet of Fort Howard, but it burnt down last Winter. I have located a Catholic Friar that is near Fort Howard. He is working among the Oneida and Menominee tribes. The only problem is, he only speaks French, Iroquoian, and Algonquin. I want a Christian wedding too. So, I went to our trading post in Green Bay, I located the friar. His name is Friar Jedidiah Moris. Our Green Bay manager, Dubois, is French Canadian and he helped me talk Friar Moris into coming down here to reside at our wedding. The friar agreed to it for a handsome donation to his Oneida ministry. Dubois offered to bring the Father down here. I hope it's all right with you. The Friar is available every weekend in August, beginning August" tenth."

Sophia interrupts with, "Our wedding will be on August tenth."

I continue, "The biggest building in town is Sullivan's barn. I hope you don't mind but, I talked to Jacob about using his barn as our wedding hall. He told me that we are welcome to use it. When I asked him, what he would charge us to use it? He said that it will be his wedding gift to us. You see I've been thinking of our wedding too my dear."

Daniel approached Jacob about buying two lots and ends up buying the entire ten-acre farm. Daniel intends to put roads in and divide the farm into residential and commercial lots. He will make a road that leads to the lots that Daniel and I will build our houses on. I jokingly make a street sign that reads, "Wells

Street" and install it at the end of the road.

Jacob and his family are moving twenty five miles north to a little community located on the shore of Lake Michigan at the mouth of Sauk Creek. The village is founded by a Revolutionary War veteran, named General Wooster Harrison. The General named his little settlement Wisconsin City.

General Harrison's House in Port Washington.

The people of Wisconsin City will starve out in the winter and be forced to walk to Milwaukee. Eight years after abandoning Wisconsin City, General Harrison and a small group including Jacob and his family, will return to Wisconsin City. It will become a successful town. Eventually the town will change its name to Port Washington.

Millie and Sophia have been busy getting ready for our wedding. They sent invitations to everyone we know including General Hull and Lieutenant Baxter at Fort Dearborn. Sophia is feeling under pressure and getting a little edgy lately. I'm seeing a new side of her, and it is a bit scary. I try to avoid her when I can these days. I'm learning that we work better apart in times like this. At the end of each day, we make time to sit on our porch together and have a glass of beer. We unwind and talk about our day. I always ask Sophia, "What was your favorite part of your day?" Our wedding is, of course, the main topic these days.

The other item that Sophia reminds me of every evening is that we have owned the lot for two weeks now and when am I going to start building our new house? I'm certain that Millie is pestering Daniel as well. Sophia doesn't know, but I talked to my Irish carpenter friends about it. They will begin building our new houses tomorrow while Daniel and I are out of town.

Daniel, George, Solomon, and I got up early to go to our new territorial capital in Belmont. It's located in the southwest part of Wisconsin. We will be traveling west on the Blue Mound trail. It takes five days to get there. We intend to meet with our newly appointed territorial governor, Henry Dodge to submit an application to purchase government land. Solomon met the Governor, during the early days of the Black Hawk war. At that time, Dodge was a Colonel serving in the Michigan State Militia. He was in command of a unit called the Michigan Mounted Volunteers.

We are traveling west on the Blue Mound trail. There are reports of Fox and Sauk Indians attacking whites on this trail. Solomon brought along a new employee named Isaac Bigelow, to have another man with a musket riding along with us.

Gratefully, this trip has been uneventful so far. At the end of our third day, we are entering Dodgeville. It was named after our governor. We decide to spend the night at the Roughly Hotel. We had dinner here at the hotel. After dinner we have a pint of ale at the bar and then we go to bed.

It's the morning of the fourth day of our trip, we stop at the hotel restaurant for some hard-boiled eggs and sausage for breakfast. We saddle our horses, and we are on our way.

While we are on the trail Solomon says, "This is how the system works. We will go to the governor's political campaign office and make a cash donation. The Governor will be notified of the donation before our meeting with him. Promptly at one o'clock we will walk into the Governor's office. An aid will meet with us and tell us that the Governor reviewed our request. Then he will put the Governor's stamp of approval on it. We will be on our way back home by two 0' clock this afternoon. That is exactly the way it worked, and we are home five days later.

We arrived home from our trip late last night. I was exhausted so Sophia and I went straight to bed. I wake up this morning to hear good news. The Irish carpenters finished our new house! I'm excited to see it so Sophia and I walk over to the house before breakfast. Sophia surprises me. She had myoid sitting stump removed. In its place she had the masons build a stone porch off of the back of our house. On the porch is a brand-new rocking chair right where the stump was located. I love that girl!

The town's women have been working hard getting ready for the wedding since I left town. They sent invitations to everyone we know, including General Hull and Lieutenant Baxter at Fort Dearborn. Sophia is feeling under pressure and getting a little edgy lately. I'm seeing a new side of her and it's scaring me a bit. I think I'll try to avoid her when I can. Hopefully myoid Sophia will be back after the wedding.

It's the fifth of August, less than a week until our wedding day. Not surprisingly, Sophia has every detail under control. Thanks to Millie and Solomon's wife, Josette, for all their help. We have had a response to our handwritten invitations from 276 people. Many of the guests are bringing food and other helpful items to the reception. The only person who didn't respond is my sister Anna. I am worried sick about her welfare. Byron Kilbourn was sent an invitation, but he declined. His associates, Allen Lapham, Archibald Clybourn and Garret Vliet are all attending though

A disparaging statement about Juneau Town, was made in Byron Kilbourn's westside partisan newspaper called, "The Milwaukee Advertiser" during Milwaukee's "Bridge War". It prompted Solomon Juneau to provide start-up funds for John O'Rourke, a former assistant editor at The Advertiser to start the Milwaukee Sentinel newspaper.

Jim O'Rourke wrote in his fledgling newspaper, The Milwaukee Sentinel. "The Gutenriemer-Kemp wedding will be held at Sullivan's barn on Wells Street in Juneau Town. The wedding will be held on August 10, 1830, at 1:00 p.m. The Gutenriemer-Kemp wedding is said by many to be the social event of the year in Wisconsin Territory."

Predictably, The Milwaukee Advertiser didn't mention our wedding. Both newspapers are giving a lot of print to the maiden voyage of the new stagecoach company on August 10. It will run between Fort Dearborn and Milwaukee. Time has flown by this past week. It's hard to believe that this is the day that the love of my life will become my wife. I chose Solomon to be my best man. Millie is Sophia's maid of honor. These two special people in our lives have stepped up and taken care of every detail for this remarkable day.

There is a crowd gathering on Water Street. Solomon says to George and I, "Let's walk over there and find out what's going on." As we approach Water Street there is a brand-new stagecoach storming up the road and then coming to an abrupt stop.

Whoa! The trailing cloud of dust is catching up, then overtaking the stagecoach. Spectators are clapping and cheering to welcome its arrival. The driver reaches down on the side of the coach, grabs hold of the brake lever and pulls it back hard until it catches. He then reaches behind him and throws a sack that has US MAIL printed in white on each side to the ground. It hits the ground in a puff of dust. The post master's assistant shuffles over to the sack, picks it up, and quickly walks back toward our new Post Office.

The driver then swings around in his seat, climbs down onto the front wheel, and hops down. He takes two steps to the coach door, pulls up on the door handle and holds the door open for the passengers to exit. The inside of the coach is dark. We can hear the passengers shuffling around in the coach as they gather their belongings.

The crowd becomes quiet, while in anticipation to see who will be the first passenger to step through the door. General Hull ducks through the door and steps down, followed by Lieutenant Baxter. Solomon and I are working our way through the crowd to greet them. Behind them is a well-dressed gentleman in his early forties.

He pokes his head out of the door as if he's looking for someone. He then steps out of the coach and pauses. He is a very poised gentleman, standing tall with a confident, but pleasant attitude. He looks to the right and then to the left. He then walks to the back of the coach to gather his luggage.

I turn back to the General to continue our conversation, then out of the corner of my eye I see Anna poking her head out of the coach door.

"Anna, I had no idea! It is so good to see you! Does Sophia know? She does, doesn't she? Its so good to see you, Anna."

A sinking feeling falls over me. "Are you okay? Is everything alright with you?"

Anna quickly responds, "We will talk about me later. I need to get cleaned up and I want to say hello to Sophia."

"Of course. I'll take you to her. Oh, how rude of me, Anna, this is my good friends George and Solomon."

Anna says, "It's good to meet both of you. Sophia and Johann have told me all about you in their letters. I'm looking forward to meeting Josette. Now I want to see Sophia."

George stays at the stagecoach with the General. Solomon and I go with Anna. When we get to my house, Anna turns to me, and puts both hands on my chest to stop me.

She lowers her eyebrows, and in an authoritarian tone of voice says, "Johann, you can't come in the house Sophia is in there. Now you go get ready for the wedding. Solomon, I will see you at one o'clock too. Solomon makes sure that he gets to the wedding on time. Now go away. I don't want you to see Sophia."

Sophia, Josette, Millie, and many other women in our town have done an amazing job cleaning and preparing Jacob's barn for our wedding. It's hard to imagine that just a few weeks ago this barn had hay on the ground piled twenty feet high. There were horse stalls and cow stanchions where the alter and seating is now. With the help of friends, I disassembled and moved the stalls and stanchions out of the barn. My Irish carpenter friends built a shed to house the cows and horses until after our wedding. The hay that was piled up in the barn was bailed and will be used as seating for our guests.

Chapter Fourteen

I'll Take You Home

George is still at the stagecoach getting Anna's luggage. The driver hands him the luggage. George waits to see who the last two men to exit the coach are. They appear to be staying in the coach until the spectators disperse. One man gets up and leans his head and shoulders out the door. He scans the area for a moment, then steps forward, and stands with one foot on the step and the other still in the coach. The man has wide shoulders and a full black beard. He is dressed in black. There are two flintlock pistols in his belt and a 16" knife sheathed on his side. He pauses for a moment longer. He now steps down and stands on the ground outside the coach with his eyes still scanning the area. He has one hand is on a pistol with his thumb on the hammer. The last man in the coach is also dressed in black. He gets up from his seat and picks up a black cape that is lying on the seat. He steps toward the door.

George hears a loud crash behind him. He spins around to see that large crates have fallen off of a freight wagon. The mules that are hitched to it spook and begin running down the street in his direction without a driver. People in the street are running for their lives in all directions to avoid being trampled by the mules.

There is a shattering scream. George sees the mule team running straight at four-year-old, little Amelia O'Rourke. Her mother helplessly watches Amelia tumbling under the mule's hooves as the team runs over her. It's over in a second. Amelia's contorted little body lies face down in the street motionless. Her mother, Bellamy runs to Amelia and falls to her knees, leans over

Amelia, and picks up her limp little girl. Bellamy is embracing little Amelia and is sobbing uncontrollably. George runs over to Bellamy and drops to his knees next to Bellamy. George puts his arm around her. After allowing Bellamy a few minutes, he helps her to her feet. She is in a state of shock as she holds her dead child. George walks the grieving mother who is carrying little Amelia to their home.

I'm at Solomon and Josette's house getting ready for our wedding. I assume that Josette is helping Sophia.

I'm at Solomon's house. I'm pacing. Why am I pacing? Not knowing about the tragedy, I think to myself, "*where the hell is George? He told me he would be here a half hour ago.*" My wedding is at 1:00 so I have only three hours until it starts. Daniel stops by with a jug of beer to see how I'm doing. It's exactly what I need. One of my best friends is at my side and a beer is in my hand.

Daniel asks in an off-the-cuff manner, "I was told that someone has been asking about you around town. Has he talked to you?"

"Who is it? I'm not aware of anyone that's looking for me. Is it General Hull or Lieutenant Baxter?"

Then, before Daniel can answer, George walks in. I ask him, "Where have you been?"

George replies, "I'll tell you about that later. I'll have a beer. Now I'll help to get you ready. You have a wedding this afternoon."

I look over at Daniel and I can see that he is distracted. I assume he's thinking about the man that's looking for me.

Solomon walks in the door. I think to myself, "Here I am with the best friends I have ever had. They are here for me on the most important day of my life. How could I be so blessed to have them?"

George looks at his watch and says, "It's 12:15. We should start thinking about going to Jacob's barn."

There's a knock on the door. Before it can be answered the door swings open. It's Millie, and she's out of breath, she promptly asks, "Have any of you seen Sophia? Josette, Anna, and I left her alone in her house while we were on the front porch, talking to the Friar. When we went back into the house, she was gone. Anna is over checking Jacob's barn for her. Where else could she be? It's not like her to just leave without letting me know where she's going. We need to be over at the barn in one half hour. I'm going back to the barn. Josette is over there, and she may have found Sophia. I'll see you all at 1:00. Guys, make sure the groom gets there on time. Don't be late."

After Millie leaves, Solomon pulls George off to the side and is talking quietly to him. While he's talking to George, I'm thinking that these guys must be planning something, I'll just leave them work on their little prank. George and Solomon look at each other and George says, "We're going to take off. We'll see you two at the barn."

It's now 12:30. Daniel and I are about to leave for the wedding. The door opens. George walks in. He is out of breath, "Johann, we can't find Sophia. She's not at Jacobs Barn and not at Millie's house. No one has seen her since twelve o'clock. Do you know where else she may be?"

Without answering I run to the barn. I'm afraid I know what happened. I have feared this since I saw the wanted poster.

George and Daniel are running behind me. When I get to the barn, I run inside. She isn't there. Guests are beginning to arrive, and they are confused.

I call out, "Sophia! Sophia! Has anyone seen Sophia?"

The town constable, JT Smith, hurries over to me to find out what's going on. After I tell him, JT asks, "Who was the last person to see her? Where have you checked for her?"

When I tell him he stands on a chair and announces, "We don't know where Sophia is. Has anyone seen Sophia?"

He waits for a response, then, when no one responds, JT requests, "We can't find Sophia. Everyone, please help us look for her. Report to me with anything you learn about her."

The guests disperse in search of Sophia. They are talking among themselves. Some are deeply concerned for Sophia's well-being. Some are confused and others seem angry that their plans for the afternoon are disrupted.

I am thinking clearly now about the stagecoach arrival. I remember that George stayed at the stagecoach when I left with Anna. I wonder if he saw the last two men that were in the stagecoach.

I ask George, "Who were those last two men in black that were in the stagecoach? Tell me what they looked like."

George described the first man and then tells me of the tragedy with little Amelia and the freight wagon. It was an understandable distraction. I really don't need to be told that Baron Gutenriemer is in town.

I sense that he is, and I will find him. I have been preparing in myself for this confrontation for a long time.

"Solomon, Daniel, George can I count on your help?"

I know the answer before I ask the question. Solomon leans

forward and tells me, "We will organize several search parties. Johann, the three of us have been preparing for this and we know that you have, too."

George says, "Sophia will leave hints so look for them. When you see JT, tell him to look for them too."

I direct Daniel, Solomon, and George, "My friends, we know what to look for.

Daniel confidently says, "Don't worry Johann, we will find her."

Those simple words give me a feeling of some assurance. I ask George, "Search Walkers Point and everything south of the Menominee River. Check for clues on the Green Bay trail. They may be going back to Fort Dearborn. Solomon, you search east of the river. Check Jauk Trail for clues. The Baron may be going north to Green Bay."

"Daniel, you're in charge of the west side of the river. Tell Byron Kilbourn that Sophia has been kidnaped. Ask for his help finding her."

Daniel replies, "Allen Lapam, is already searching the west side of the river."

Another one of Kilbourn's employees, Garret Vliet is searching the Waukesha Road and will put the word out in Waukesha. Solomon's friend, Archibald Cylbourn, is looking for Sophia on the Fond Du Lac Trail.

General Hull sent a rider to alert Major Zachary Taylor at Fort Howard, near Green Bay, asking him to watch for Sophia and the Baron. Then he ordered the Lieutenant to return to Fort Dearborn and send detachments to search Racine and Waukesha. Everyone in Milwaukee has been notified of Sophia's kidnapping. Hundreds of people have been searching for more than two hours without success. The Baron, his bodyguard, and Sophia could be twenty miles away by now.

Every building in Walkers Point, Kilbourn Town, and Juneau Town has been checked. The only posse leader that has not checked in with me is JT Smith.

I am worried sick about Sophia's safety. I'm doing everything I can to keep my emotions under control and stay focused on finding Sophia.

I meet up with Solomon and Daniel.

Daniel says, "We have taken a shotgun approach up until now, and that was the proper way for us to attack this problem. Now, let's focus on the Baron's potential escape route and track him like a bloodhound. It's time to approach this as detectives. Let's start at the last place Sophia was seen. Gentlemen, Let's go to Johann's house."

When we arrive at my house, Solomon says, "Don't touch anything. Johann, has anyone been in this house since Sophia was abducted?"

I reply, "No."

Daniel enters first and lights an oil lamp. When we enter the front door, we can see that the back door has been left open. One of our bentwood chairs is laying down on its side. Millie's pewter teapot is on the floor near the back door. There is a little dried blood on the spout. I point out that the dining table is moved about two feet from where it was. Someone had to have pushed it or bumped into it. The back porch has large partially dried drops of blood in a line from the backdoor stoop across the porch to the backyard. The blood trail continues across the backyard to the lake bluff. We lost the blood trail down the bluff in the dark. Further down the bluff Daniel finds an area where damp clay had been disturbed recently. There are boot tracks heading down toward the beach.

When we get to the bottom of the bluff, Solomon finds three sets of boot tracks on the beach that are ten inches long and one set of seven-inch tracks between them. They are walking to the north.

There are at least a hundred people searching for Sophia in every possible place in Milwaukee. We also widened our search outside of town to the north, west, and south. Because of Lake Michigan, no one considered looking to the east. If Sophia or one of her captors were not injured and left a blood trail, we wouldn't have thought of searching to the east. I should have listened to myself when I said, "*Sophia will lead us to her. Look for her clues.*"

The moon is almost full, aiding us in following the trail. We are also fortunate that the wind is from the west, so waves haven't washed their tracks away. I'm surprised that the Baron hadn't considered that he is leaving such an obvious trail. It's not like him to make a mistake.

Solomon avows his concern, "The Baron's bodyguard is carrying two pistols and a sixteen-inch blade. We must assume that the Baron is carrying a pistol as well. We are completely unarmed. I don't want to come upon the Baron in the dark when we don't have a weapon. We won't be able to continue tonight. We can take up the chase in the morning. Daniel, go tell JT that we found the Baron's trail. Ask JT to meet us at my house tomorrow morning at first light and to bring some armed men."

Solomon adds, "I'll talk to Alex Stuart. He has some coon and bear hound dogs that could follow the Baron's trail."

George says, "No dogs. If the hears the hounds chasing him, and he's cornered, it could turn this into a hostage situation."

Daniel hurries to the jailhouse hoping to find JT or someone that may know where he is. As he is approaching the jail, Daniel sees a crowd standing around next door at the courthouse.

Shockingly, he finds JT lying on a table with a musket ball through his stomach and his throat slit open from ear to ear. "Who did it? (Although he already knew) "Where did it happen?"

JT was a likable kind of guy. Daniel had become very close to JT in the short time that they had known each other. Daniel's first reaction is instinctively, anger. "That son-of-a-bitch! It was Baron von Gutenriemer or his damn henchman! Is there anyone that will join Johann, Solomon, George, and me? We have found their trail. They have Sophia. We are going to hunt that murdering son-of-a-bitch down and hang them. Meet us in the morning at daybreak at Solomon Juneau's house. Bring your muskets."

One-half hour before first light the four of us, plus JT's brother named Cornelius meet on the front porch. Solomon says, "No one else is coming. Let's head out to where we saw the last sign of the Baron's trail."

When we get there it's light. I see a small piece of white lace laying on the ground fifty paces up the trail. I point it out to the other men. "Sophia was here." I say, Then I think to myself, *"hold on a little longer Sophia. I'm on my way!"*

The hard ground in the forest is making it difficult to follow the baron's trail. Sophia is leaving signs such as a broken branch or fern when she can. Occasionally we see subtle signs such as leaves turned up on the ground, indicating that Sophia has passed this way.

Solomon points out three places where the grass and leaves

are patted down and says, "They had bedded down here."

He points out a hair clip laying on one of the patted down places. Daniel bends over picks up a hair clip and says, "Millie was letting Sophia wear this at her wedding then puts it in his pocket.

Solomon says, "I think that they're about ten or hours ahead of us. The due has been dripping off the trees this morning. Check the powder on your muskets. Make sure that it is dry."

As we're walking, I am telling the men about the Baron, "Daniel, you know this, but it's important that the others understand the Baron von Gutenriemer. He has wealth and power beyond your imagination. For generations my family lived on his family's land and in his laborer's cottage. We were serfs living under his rule. While we were living on his property, he controlled every part of our lives. I have seen the Baron many times, but I have never met him."

"I should have told you this before. Sophia is the Baron's daughter. You must understand, it's not like any father daughter relationship that you've ever known. There has never been any love between the two of them. I'm sure that he is incapable of love. After studying the Baron for the last two years, I am convinced that he is incapable of loving anyone. He considers Sophia to be his property, such as his land, cattle, and indentured servants. He thinks nothing of killing anyone that attempts to take anything he owns away from him. I have come to realize that in his mind, I took Sophia away from him. I'm certain that when I take her back, there will be a price on my head. He will put out a bounty for the four of you as my accomplices. Knowing this, I understand if you men want to go home."

There is silence as they look at each other and then they look at me. Solomon walks over to me, puts his hand on my shoulder, and then speaks, "Johann I can speak for all of us. We aren't going to walk out on you and Sophia. As I see it, our only way out of this is that, when we rescue Sophia, we will have to eliminate the Baron and his bodyguard."

He looks at each of us waiting for an objection. "Okay, now let's pick up the pace."

As we are following the Baron's trail, I keep thinking about what Solomon said to me. I have known all along that I will have to confront the Baron at some point. The thought scares the Hell out of me. He is a very smart and deliberate person. He has had a plan in everything that I have seen him do in his business dealings. If the plan didn't work out, he always had a contingency plan. And, he always ends up winning in the end.

The Baron is now heading southwest through the forest. Where is he going? Ultimately, I know that he is going back to his home in Mecklenburg. The question is what route is he taking?

The Baron is a man of means and he is accustomed to traveling in comfort. There just isn't a carriage in Wisconsin Territory that will meet his standards. That's it! I think he's going to Isaac Bigelow's Wagon Works in Waukesha. He had a wagon built for himself. The Baron knows that he won't be able to drive back through Milwaukee and Chicago because he would be recognized. He has two other options. He can either travel north to Green Bay and board an eastbound schooner across Lake Michigan. Or his other option is to head west on Blue Mound Military trail to Fort Prairie du Chien. From there he could board a riverboat and go down the Mississippi River, to New Orleans. In New Orleans he can board a clipper ship for England, and then on to Mecklenburg.

I just realized that Baron von Gutenriemer met my sister and General Hull on the stagecoach trip between Fort Dearborn and

Milwaukee. They road together for two days. I am sure that sometime during their conversations that, ether Anna or General Hull mentioned that the reason for their trip was to attend our wedding. Hearing that his daughter is marrying a commoner must have infuriated the baron.

When I lived under the Baron's rule, it was common knowledge that he would imprison or execute anyone that stole from him. There was never a trial like we have here in America.

The Baron is consistent when it comes to his policy on punishing those who steal his property. He will hunt down the perpetrator at any cost. He's been known to have taken ten years and travel hundreds of miles to hunt down and punish an offender.

I am confident that he will send an executioner for me. I won't know who it is, I won't know when or where he or she will appear. I do know that his punishment is certain. His henchmen may be hunting me down at this moment.

When we arrive in Waukesha and talk with Isaac Bigelow. Isaac informs us that no one had picked up a wagon today. He says that he heard about Sophia's abduction, and offers his condolences. He goes on to say that he is on the lookout for Sophia.

As we are talking, he says, "Wait a moment, I do remember talking to someone that wanted to buy a wagon last week. He was insistent that he had to have it within a week. When I told the man that with my existing orders that it would be impossible. He said he would have to get one elsewhere. I told him to try Murphy's Stable, you should check with Murphy. I can tell you that the man that was looking for the wagon spoke German. He carried a pistol tucked in his belt. No, he had two pistols in his belt. That was so unusual for our little town."

We thank Isaac and go over to Murphy's stable. Murphy tells us that he did sell a customized carriage and a team of geldings. He brags, "The guy gave me a $20 gold piece. to have the team fed, watered, and hitched up by 6:00 this morning. Hell, I would have done it for twenty cents!"

We thank Isaac and go over to Murphy's stable. Murphy tells us that he did sell a customized carriage and a team of geldings. He brags, "The guy gave me a $20 gold piece. to have the team fed, watered, and hitched up by 6:00 this morning. Hell, I would have done it for twenty cents!"

Murphy goes on to say, "The man was alone. He went trotting west, on Blue Mound Road. As I think about it, I did see him stop and pick up two people at the hotel on his way out of town."

I ask, "Was one of the people that he picked up a woman?"

Murphy said that it was a distance down the road but one of them was shorter and probably could have been a woman."

We lease five horses with saddles and bridles from Murphy and we were on the Baron's trail by midday.

As we are trotting down the road, I'm thinking that I don't understand why JT was killed. I speed up until I'm riding next to Solomon, and I say, "I can't figure out why JT was murdered. What's your take on it? Do you know where JT was murdered?"

Solomon takes a moment while he chooses his words. He spits his tobacco and says, "You know Johann, that's been bothering me too. I've put a lot of thought to it. Why JT? He was shot from behind. It appeared that after shooting JT, the murderer walked up behind him and slit his throat. The cut and blood stains indicate that he was slashed from his right to his left. That tells me that his murderer is left-handed. The killer took the time to stand over JT and watch him die lying face down. He then

190

wiped the blood off both sides of his blade on JT's shoulder. This man has killed before. An amateur would have shot him in the back and run away. Johann, I think JT's murderer took joy in killing our friend. You asked where he was killed? JT was killed on his way to your house last night. He is the same size as you and was wearing a black suit just like the one you were wearing yesterday. I think JT's murderer thought that he had killed you!"

Back in Milwaukee, Millie has invited Josette to stay at her house while their husbands are away. They are in the house talking about yesterday's events. Although they are close friends and talk to each other daily, Josette is a very private person. She seldom talks about herself. Today, Josette professes to Millie that her mother is from the Menominee Indian tribe.

Millie responds, "You should be proud of your heritage, Josette. I sensed that you have some Indian blood in you. You have those beautiful black eyes and straight black hair. You're a beautiful woman, and your mother must have been beautiful too."

Josette then tells Millie that she is twenty-seven years younger than Solomon. Millie tries to keep her composure when hearing it. Her mature personality and weathered complexion make her seem much older than she is. Josette's hard life has aged her beyond her years.

There is a knock on the door. The ladies look at each other. "Are you expecting anyone? Are the men back?"

"No, it's not Daniel's knock."

Millie gets up from her chair and walks to the fireplace. She looks over her shoulder at Josette as she reaches for the musket that's hanging over the mantle. Without a word being said Josette stands up and walks over to her and is waiting for the gun. Millie turns and hands it to her. The women look at each other for a second, then turn to the door together. With the muzzle pointed down, Josette pulls the hammer back, and raises the musket barrel at the door.

Millie walks to the door. She glances over her shoulder at Josette then slides the door latch back and slowly opens the door, just enough to peek around the edge to see who is on the other side, "Papa? Papa? Papa!"

Millie swings the door wide open. She runs through the doorway and hugs the man who's standing on her front porch around his arms, knocking him off balance.

She asks, "I'm so happy you're here! What a wonderful surprise! I missed you so much! Why didn't you write Daddy? Why didn't you let me know that you were coming?"

Millie's father responds, "I missed you too my darling Millicent. You look quite healthy my dear. I see you've been eating well. Aren't you going to introduce me to your friend?"

Millie responds, "Oh, of course. This is my dear friend Josette Juneau. She lives down the street. Josette, this is my father, Casper von Voght. He's my papa if you hadn't already guessed. He arrived from Hamburg, Mecklenburg."

Casper holds his hand out, "It's a pleasure to meet you, Josette." Then turning his head to Millie, "Well where is my son-in-law, Daniel? Is he away on business?"

Millie replies, "Yes, Daniel is away for a while. I'll fill you in on it. First, come in and bring your luggage. Are you hungry? When did you arrive in Milwaukee? Would you like a glass of beer?"

Millie begins walking to the second bedroom, in a sad tone, she says, "I was so sorry to hear in your last letter about Grobmutter. I think about her almost every day. You will stay in this room Daddy. I think of Mother too. I miss her so much."

"I miss her too Millicent. It will be seven years next month," He pauses, "I'll take that beer you offered me."

Josette is looking at Millie's father and wondering, "*This man looks familiar. Where have I seen him before?*"

After putting his stateroom trunk in the bedroom Casper comes out of the bedroom and says, "Let's sit out on the back deck where we can look over Lake Michigan while we talk."

Millie replies, "Splendid. Josette, please join us on the deck.

I'll get a jug of beer and some mugs for us."

The three of them spend the entire afternoon visiting on the deck, Casper is telling stories of times when Millie was young in Hamburg and laughing about it. Josette is mostly listening. She is a bit envious of Millie's childhood. You see, Josette's father died when she was just a baby. He was killed in The War of 1812 fighting as an ally of the British, against American troops. Her mother died of smallpox when Josette was three years old. She was then adopted by a family in her tribe who really never treated Josette like part of their family. Josette was beaten often and severely by her adoptive parents for the smallest infractions. When she met Solomon, she was just fourteen years old and fell in love with him. Solomon offered a handsome dowery to Josette's adoptive parents for their daughter's hand in marriage and it was accepted. Solomon and Josette have been together ever since.

Casper asks, "Millicent, in your letter you said that Daniel wanted to talk to me about a business venture concerning buying United States federal land here in Wisconsin Territory for logging timber. Daniel is aware that I am always looking for opportunities to buy cheap land in America. It sounds like something that I would be interested in. I'm here to talk about it. When will Daniel return from his business trip?"

Millie takes a sip of beer then tells her father about Sophia's kidnapping and how Daniel is helping Johann rescue her. She talks about Sophia's father and where he came from. Millie begins telling her father all about Baron von Gutenriemer's pursuit of Sophia and how he came all the way from Mecklenburg to Milwaukee. She explains that Daniel is pursuing Baron von Gutenriemer to get Sophia back.

Casper interrupts Millie. "Okay, I've heard enough. I understand what you're saying. I've known the Baron for many years."

Josette perks up and says, "That's where I saw you! You came out of the stagecoach yesterday. You were riding with Anna, the General and those two strangers, weren't you?"

Casper answers, "That's right. It was I on the stagecoach. The two strangers you are speaking of are the Baron von Gutenriemer and his bodyguard/assassin named Brutus."

"I spent two days with the five passengers you speak of. The five of us talked and got to know each other well. Although Gutenriemer and his bodyguard didn't say much at all. He is

 an angry man. He's determined to get his property back. Although, he didn't say that the property that he was talking about is his daughter. When talking to me privately he said that he was going to execute the thief that stole from him."

Casper goes on to say, "When I arrived in town yesterday, I contacted the town's law enforcement officer and told him of my conversation with the Baron. I think that Constable Smith was ambushed by Brutus and murdered on his way to alert Mr. Kemp of his peril. Brutus then would have reported back to Baron von Gutenriemer that Mr. Kemp was killed."

Millie adds, "Baron von Gutenriemer left town with Sophia right after the murder so he couldn't have any idea that Brutus killed the wrong man."

Danial sent word to me that, the Baron, Brutus, and Sophia are traveling in an enclosed carriage pulled by a two-horse team. Brutus is driving and the Baron and Sophia are riding comfortably inside the coach. The baron ordered locks to be installed on the doors and wrought iron bars over the windows to make the coach a traveling jail cell. Indeed, a very comfortable jail cell, with soft tufted leather seats and plush carpeted floor. The windows have black shads that always remain drawn.

Sophia is a clever and resourceful. She is constantly looking for a flaw in her father's plans. For now, though, escape appears to be futile. The Baron is seated facing forward. Sophia is sitting across from him. Sophia has been looking at the floor since she sat down. She has avoided all eye contact since the moment that she was captured.

Inside the coach is very dark with the only light entering through the small space around the edges of the black window shades. Sophia is feeling like a captured animal that had escaped. It has been caught and is now being transported back to a life of captivity.

The Baron is sitting in the seat across from Sophia. He is silently reveling in the thought that he had the man that took his daughter away from him executed. the Baron is anxiously awaiting the moment when he tells Sophia that he had her fiancé executed.

Baron von Gutenriemer is traveling at a casual pace. He's assuming that the only person that has a serious incentive to pursue him and Sophia was killed by his assassin, Brutus. In the late afternoon Brutus calls down to the Baron and tells him that they are entering the town of Jefferson. The Baron opens the window shade and orders Brutus to stop at a hotel.

The Baron checks into the Jefferson House Hotel and orders Brutus to drive outside of town and find a place for he and Sophia to camp for the night.

Then he tells Brutus, "Keep Sophia locked in the carriage. Pick me up here at the hotel at 8:00 in the morning."

Brutus climbs up into the driver's seat, grabs a hold of the reins. Then he slaps the horses butt with the reins and orders, "Get up!"

He turns the carriage around in the street and drives out of town. When he gets about two miles out of town, he pulls off the road near a stream. Sophia can hear Brutus, unhitching, and watering the horses. There are footsteps walking toward the carriage. Sophia hears a key entering the door lock and unlocking the door. Now the door opens sunlight enters the carriage and it's blinding. Brutus stands outside for a moment. A smile is forming on his face. He climbs into the carriage and leans forward onto Sophia. She is fighting him with every bit of strength she has, but resistance is pointless when a 250-pound man is on top of a 120-pound girl. Brutus rips Sophia's clothing off and rapes her. Brutus returns two more times, later in the evening.

Brutus is waiting with the carriage in front of the hotel at 8:00 AM for the Baron to complete his breakfast. At 8:20 the Baron walks out of the hotel, puts his ruby studded dagger and in a breast sheath and climbs into the carriage. He briefly glances at Sophia in her torn clothing and then looks forward expressionless. The Baron leans toward the window and orders, "Let's go driver."

Back at the Millie's house, Casper is sleeping in the second bedroom, so Josette moved her things into Millie and Daniel's bedroom. Millie and Josette are early risers, and they are both awake at first light.

Josette whispers: "Millie, are you awake?"

"Yes, I am. I'm just lying here thinking about Daniel and Solomon. I'm so worried"

Josette replies, "I'm thinking of them too. I think that I'll get up and go over to my house. There are some things that I need to do. I'll let you have some time alone with your father today."

Millie replies, "Thank you. I've missed him so much. I know what he's going to want to do though. He's going to want to talk business. I run the business side of Daniel's company, so sadly, we will be working today. That's okay though, it will help to keep my mind off of worrying about Daniel."

Josette slides out of bed and gets dressed. "I smell coffee brewing. Your father is up. I'll be back at supper time."

Millie gets out of bed and goes into the kitchen.

"Good morning, Millicent. Pour yourself a cup of coffee. I've been thinking of the logging business. There is an opportunity for us to make a lot of money here! After you have breakfast, I want to ride with you up to the land that Daniel is talking about buying. I'd like to open a bank here in Milwaukee as well. The only bank in this town is owned by Byron Kilbourn and I don't think that I want to deal with him. Millicent, please investigate the Wisconsin Territorial regulations concerning licensing required to open a bank. Is there an attorney in town? Do you have a survey map of the land that Daniel is interested in? Your letter indicated that there is a gentleman named Juneau that will handle the shipping is that Josette's husband? I'd like to meet him. Millicent, are you writing all this down?"

In pursuit of Sophia, we find ourselves in a little Welsh community named Wales. It's a very welcoming community. There seems to be about thirty families living here. Solomon speaks enough English to rent a room above the saloon and make arrangements to keep our horses in the barn next door. After putting away the horses, we have a pint of ale at the bar.

Solomon asks the saloon keeper what he's serving for dinner.

He replies, "Crawl and Bara."

We look at each other in hopes that one of us knows what it is. We haven't eaten all day, so we order it. When arrives at the bar we find it to be a stew with venison and vegetables. There is also a fruity bread that the bartender calls Bara. The stew and fruit bread are delicious!

In the morning of our second day on the Baron's trail. Cornelius wakes up with a severe pain in his Abdomen. After we determine that it's not food poisoning from the crawl or bara. We decide that the pain is appendicitis. Appendicitis is not treatable. Nothing is said but we all know that most people don't survive it. It's a painful death. The only treatment for it is to take morphine for the pain.

We are talking about our options and decide to hire someone to take Cornelius back to his home in Milwaukee. By the time we find someone it's midday.

The last words that I hear Cornelius say as he is carried away on a wagon are, "Kill that sun-of-a-bitch for me!"

There is not even one word spoken between Sophia and the Baron today. Sophia is being treated like a trophy animal that was hunted down, captured, and caged. It's 3:00 when the Baron orders Brutus to stop at the Hotel Monona in Madison Town. Brutus pulls the Coach up to the curb in front of the hotel entrance. He swings out of the driver's seat, steps down onto the front wheel, then jumps down to the ground and hurries to the coach door. He opens it and stands at attention holding the door for the Baron.

Gutenriemer orders, "Lock the door and get my luggage down for me. Then carry it to the cashier's desk. After that, I want you to drive the coach out of town and find a camp site for the evening. Make sure you are back here at eight o'clock in the morning.

In the morning, Brutus has the carriage waiting in front of the hotel at 7:45. Brutus holds the door open for the Baron as he enters the Carriage. The Baron glances at Sophia as he takes his seat. She has dried blood under her nose and a bruise under her eye.

The Baron opens the shade and orders, "You may proceed driver."

Solomon, George, and Daniel are amazing friends of mine. I couldn't have gotten this far without them. We have been traveling for ten hours today and pushing the horses harder than we did yesterday. It's time to a rest them. We'll stop and set up camp next to this stream.

There is a trapper's cabin next to the stream. The owner sees us stop and he comes out to greet us. He recognizes Solomon from years back when Solomon had a trading post in the town of Portage on the Wisconsin River.

"Solomon, do you remember me? I am Jean Lapage."

They talk for a while and then I ask Solomon to ask the trapper if he has seen the Baron's carriage.

Solomon asks, "Oui j' ai fait..." ("Have you seen a black, carriage that is being pulled by a team of white geldings?")

Jean answers, "Une voiture noire a une herure..."

I look at Solomon who says, "He said that he saw the carriage at one o'clock today. It was westbound traveling at a casual trot." He continues, "There are bars on the windows. Jean said that he's never seen anything like it."

Jean invites us to join him for opossum stew and we oblige him. After dinner, the trapper asked us to join him in a cup or two of his home-brewed gin. Of course, we couldn't refuse his hospitality.

I wake up and it's the first light in the morning. The trapper's gin and listening to his funny stories last night was a needed relief on this very stressful trip.

Solomon sits up in his sleeping cot looks at me and says, "Jean's information leads me to think that we are closing in on the Baron and his bodyguard. We may even confront him today. When the opportunity presents itself, we must first eliminate the bodyguard first. Whichever of us is in the position must kill him.

George speaks up, "We must assume that the Baron is riding inside the carriage with Sophia. He will hold Sophia hostage to protect his own life.

Solomon gives a subtle nod in agreement as he is rolling-up his sleeping blanket and continues, "We will have to draw the Baron out of the carriage when the time comes. Check your muskets, make sure your powder is dry. Let's saddle-up. Jean isn't awake yet. We will say goodbye when we come back through.

We have been riding on the Baron's trail for two hours. Meanwhile, Brutus is waiting in front of Hotel Monona with the carriage and Sophia who is locked inside. When the Baron exits the hotel, Brutus briskly hops off the driver's seat, climbs down off the carriage and opens the door for the Baron. The Baron grabs on to the handle that is next to the door with his left hand and holds on to his pistol that is tucked in his belt with his other hand and then climbs into the carriage. He sits down without a word being said. He glances at his daughter briefly. Her hair is a mess, and she has new bruises. One on her forehead and another under her left eye. He opens the window shade just enough to order Brutus to get going.

Sophia's father is looking at her this morning in a way that is making her feel uncomfortable. She quickly looks down and continues to look at the floor. Sophia is exhausted from a night of repeated abuse. After a few minutes, curiosity causes her to look up at her father. He's still looking at her. His depressingly empty eyes are focused on her breasts. His eyebrows are slowly lowering, and a sinister smile is slowly forming on his mouth.

Sophia is fearing, *Oh my God no! What is he thinking? This can't be happening to me. You're my father for Christ's sake!* With tears forming in her eyes, she pleads out loud, "Daddy please don't! Don't do what you're thinking about!"

"Come over here, my dear. I want to touch you. I'll be gentle with you. I won't hurt you, my dear child. Come to me, my sweet little girl. Come to your daddy." He pauses for a moment then says, "Okay my dear, then I will come to you" The Baron gets up from his seat and reaches toward Sophia and tears off the top of her torn dress. He grabs Sophia's breasts with both of his hands.

As she is pushing him away with all her strength, she's pleading, "Daddy no! Daddy, please don't. She can't keep him off her, he's just too heavy. With both hands pushing on his chest, she feels her father's breast sheath. Sophia slides her hand up the sheath to the dagger handle. Wrapping her hand around it she quietly slides the dagger out of its sheath. Her father pushes himself off her a bit. While looking into each other's eyes, Sophia plunges the dagger deep into her father's left ear with all of her might. His eyes open wide with astonishment as he's pulling his head back.

Sophia can see the ruby studded handle protruding from the side of her father's head. Blood is beginning to run down the side of his face. The Baron looks into Sophia's eyes, coughs once, and mutters, "You've killed me, my dear." Then, his eyes open wide and roll up. He collapses on top of Sophia motionless. Warm blood is streaming onto Sophia's face.

Exhausted, Sophia is trying with all of her strength to move this two-hundred-and-fifty-pound corpse off of her but is unable to. After resting for a minute, she finds the strength to slide out from under her father's lifeless body. She crawls over to the other seat and turns around and looks at her father. Blood continues to drip from his ear and mouth. A narrow stream of light is coming through the window and making one of the rubies on the dagger handle sparkle.

She's staring at her father. He's lying face down on the seat in a pool of blood. His knees are on the floor. He suddenly jerks, making Sophia let out a scream. She is looking at him. There is no other movement. Sophia whispers, "You bastard. You Damn bastard! Burn in Hell Daddy!

Sophia collapses face down on her knees sobbing. She can feel the carriage slowing down. Brutus is talking to the hoses, whoa, whoa boys. The carriage comes to a stop.

Brutus calls out, "Are you alright sir?" There is silence. With no answer, he asks again, "Is everything okay sir?"

There is silence. Sophia can hear the hand break being pulled back. The driver's seat makes a squeaking sound. The carriage rocks to the right now it jerks back. She can hear Brutus step down on the front wheel and then jump to the ground. There are steps walking to the door. Now silence…. There is a knock on the door.

"Sir." Now silence as he's waiting for an answer. In a concerned tone of voice, "Sir are you alright in there?" Again silence.

Panic comes over Sophia. She's thinking, *Where can I go? There is no place hide!*

Brutus calls out, "Sir? Are you alright sir?" Brutus pauses and then says, "I'm coming in sir." Again, there is a pause. Now a metallic sound of keys on a key ring. There is a loud knock on the door. He waits a moment and then knocks again. In a loud voice, "Sir are you alright?"

Frantic ally Sophia grabs the other door latch and pulls on it. It's locked. Sophia can hear the sound of a key entering the door latch. She thinks, *Father had a pistol. Where is his pistol?*

Frantically, Sophia reaches under the Baron's limp body and pulls out his pistol. She can see the door latch turning. Her hands are shaking as she is thinking, *I've never shot one of these. It must be the same as shooting a musket. I can do this.* She points the gun at the door and pulls the hammer back.

The door begins to open, and then stops. Brutus announces, "I'm coming in sir. Did you hear me, sir?" There is a sliver of light coming through the edge of the door. Brutus draws his 16" knife. "One last time, I'm opening the door." He then swings the door open. His eyes are contracted from the bright sunny day, so he is straining to see inside the dark coach.

Sophia is blinded by the bright light. All she can see is Brutus's large black silhouette standing at the door. **BOOM!** A 45-caliber musket ball slams into the center of the assailant's forehead. The shot knocks his head back. Brutus falls on his back, with his head hitting the ground first. When the smoke clears, Sophia cautiously leans forward, and pokes her head out the carriage door to see Brutus lying on his back, spread eagle. His eyes are wide open, staring at the sky. There is a round hole in the center of his with blood spurting in a slow pumping action. Blood is running down both sides of his head forming dark red pools on the ground.

I hear a gunshot at a distance down the road. I immediately spur my horse, slap his butt, as I holler, yah! My horse is at a full run as I turn the corner to see a black carriage parked. I come riding up to it hard at a full run. Danial, George, and Solomon are right behind me. When I get to the carriage I pull back hard on the reins, jump off my horse and grab my musket. I run to the back of the carriage and stop. My gun is on my shoulder as I poke my head around the carriage. I see the door wide open. I see a man lying down, he appears to be dead. Danial and Solomon poke their heads around the other side of the carriage. I hear a hammer click behind me and I quickly turn to see George behind me.

With my gun on my shoulder, Whit my back against the carriage I quietly approach the open door. Now I quickly step in front of the door and point my gun into the carriage. Anticipating finding Baron Von Gutenriemer in the carriage with a gun pointing at the door. It is so dark in there that I can't see a thing. There is no movement in there. Now I'm starting to be able to see a large man in a black suit kneeling on the floor and laying on the seat. Across from him is my darling Sophia, slumped forward, face down on her knees. She isn't moving! Dropping my gun, I quickly climb into the coach and grab Sophia on her shoulders and lean her back on the seat. Her eyes are closed but I feel her shaking.

"Sophia, it's me, Johann. You are safe now" expressionless, she slowly raises her head and then turns to me. I quietly say, "They can't hurt you. I'll take care of you." I glance down at the Baron and see the dagger protruding from his head as I gently left her out of the carriage. Then, I lift her up in my arms, turn, and step over the dead bodyguard. I carry her away and carefully set her down on the ground under a large oak tree and kneel down next to her. Sophia turns to me and begins crying hysterically. I lean forward and hold on to her. She starts shaking uncontrollably. George brings a blanket to Sophia. He unfolds it and gently wraps it around her bare shoulders.

George then goes to help Solomon and Daniel unhitch the horses and hobble them. They drag the dead bodies deep into the woods and take all identification off of them. The men push the carriage off the trail and set it on fire. Sophia sits up with her back against the oak tree and we watch the carriage burn down to it's axles.

Danial walks over to us and says, "I'm sorry but, we must leave now before someone comes by. While the carriage was burning, Solomon made a hackamore bridle out of rope for one of the geldings. he put a blanket on the gelding he will and ride it. Sophia can ride his horse. Now let's go home."

Chapter Fifteen

Mequonsippi

We are arriving back in Milwaukee. As we are crossing the river on the ferry the bell begins ringing at the landing. Our friends are gathering on the landing and along the shore. We can hear them cheering. Many more are coming down the road to meet us. Us men look at each other and step to the back of the ferry so that Sophia can be seen by everyone. I watch Sophia slowly walk to the front railing. She reaches for the railing with both hands and holds onto it. Tears begin forming in her eyes and are streaming down her cheeks. I see that these neighbors of ours are returning the love that she has for them all.

The ferry reaches the dock and Sophia steps off onto shore. Her face is still wearing the cuts, bruises, and black eye. The gaping cut on her upper lip is scabbed over. She is wearing my shirt over her torn dress. People continue to come to the dock. Sophia is walking through the crowd, thanking, and hugging each and every person.

When I get off the ferry is to ask the first person I see how Cornelius is doing. Sadly, I'm told that his appendix burst this morning and he died.

Millie is not here at the landing. When I ask around where they are up north viewing the land that Daniel wants to log. They had no way of knowing that we arrived today. Millie's father Casper was pleased to see that the property was mainly high land. There are huge virgin hard wad trees, mainly consisting of oak, maple, and elm trees.

Casper tells Millie that he thinks a pier could be built into Lake Michigan. If it can be built, then lumber could be shipped to eastern markets. Casper says, Millicent, make a note to talk to Solomon about the feasibility of building a pier. When Danial gets back we must talk about finding a good foreman for the logging crews. Make a note that we will need to talk about running ads in eastern newspapers to hire loggers.

Millie interrupts and says, "It's getting late Daddy. Let's go back home. I want to see if Daniel has gotten back home. It will take us two hours to get there so let's get started.

As for our wedding. With all that Sophia had been through, we agreed to put the wedding off for a while. But we promised each other that we will get married as soon as we are ready to.

Six months have passed since Sophia's abduction. It is December and there is two feet of snow on the ground.

Since I saw him last, Solomon had met an attorney from Green Bay named Morgan Martin, they became friends and business partners. They have partnered in real estate development ventures. Solomon has preemption claims on valuable federal lands. Martin has expertise in real estate law and land sales. company and they are extremely successful.

Solomon is very philanthropic with his recently earned wealth. He donated the land and much of the materials to build our new town hall, courthouse, and jail building. It will replace the old one-room log building that was being used for the town hall and jailhouse until now.

George Walker
1811 - 1866

My good friend George Walker was born in Lynchburg, Virginia. Recently, he has fallen into financial despair. George had over-leveraged his real estate development in Walker's Point and lost much of his holdings to the Kilbourn Bank.

George is now representing Milwaukee in the fourth Legislative Assembly or the Wisconsin Territorial Government. He will be elected to be Milwaukee's fifth and seventh mayor.

George is a big man. He weighs more than three hundred and fifty pounds. He loves to dance, and he is very good at it. He can be seen on the dance floor with his wife, Caroline at every dance event. For a man of his size, he is truly elegant and graceful.

It's now May, nine months since we rescued Sophia from the Baron. Baron Von Gutenriemer and his bodyguard Brutus. So much has happened since then. They are a distant memory.

Millie's Casper had left for Hamburg back in September and hopefully had arrived safely. Danial is now spending most of his time managing the new Wells Bank.

Daniel made an offer to buy The Firean House Hotel and the land that Sophia owns around it from Sophia. It is a fair price, and she is going to accept his offer. Danial told her that he intends to build a new hotel on its site.

Danial has begun logging on the Northwest corner of the land that he bought from the federal government last fall. He asked me to be his foreman for the logging crews and I told him that I would accept the job until he can find a man to take over permanently. The Irish carpenters are building a bunk house and a mess hall for the loggers.

I'm running ads for laborers in New York, Boston, and Baltimore. I'm hoping to hire eight, six-man logging crews. Most important to me, is that I have found a qualified forman. He will start in two weeks.

Today is my first day on the job with the first two logging crews that I hired. After I get the crews started working, I find myself drawn to walk over to the Lake Michigan bluff. I'm standing at the edge of the bluff and looking at the magnificent lake. I can't take my eyes off of it! I'm thinking that, since I was a child, my dream was to have my own land. This is the destination that I envisioned when I set out to find my own land, three years ago! I had a vision of this place before I knew anything like this existed. I bend over and scoop up a handful of soil. Then I put the soil to my nose to smell it. It is moist, black, and smells sweet. I'm thinking, *this soil has never been turned over by a plow blade. I want to be the first man to plant and harvest a crop on this soil. I must bring Sophia up here and show her this amazing property!*

I hurry back to make sure that the crews have everything they need to continue working for the rest of the day. Then I go to the logger's camp, saddle, and bridle my horse, Bootsie. Now I'm on my way home at a brisk gallop to tell Sophia that I found our forever home today! She will be so excited to see it! As I'm riding home I'm thinking, *By the time I get back home, it will be too late to bring Sophia back up there today. We'll ride up to show her the land first thing tomorrow morning. I can't wait to see her face when she sees that land!*

Then I think, *"But, wait a minute Johann, what if she doesn't like it as much as I do? I know she really likes Milwaukee. She loves our new house. She loves living near her best friend, Millie. She just said the other day that she was so happy with our new house now that we have it set up, just the way we like it. She loves the people in Milwaukee. How can I ask her to give all of that up and move up into the wilderness? Why would I even ask her to give up her business?"*

As I'm riding along, I think of our home. It's our first house that we have owned together. Just a moment, do I really want to leave it? My best friends are living in Milwaukee. I would miss walking down to the corner saloon and having a beer with my buddies. I may have to think about this some more.

When I get to town, I go to Sophia and Adela's brewery hoping that Sophia will be there.

The brewer, Jacob Best tells me that Adela is very sick. She hasn't come to the brewery all week. Adela has had a persistent cough for two weeks, and now there is blood in her sputum. She has no appetite, and she has lost at least ten pounds.

This morning, Doc Thierman diagnosed Adela as having tuberculosis. Jacob says, "Sophia is probably at Adela's house."

I jog over there. When I arrive, Sophia is at Adela's bedside. Doc Thierman is on the other side of the bed. As I walk into the room, Sophia sees me, and a tear forms in her left eye and runs down the side of her face. Adela is sleeping quietly. There are traces of dried blood on Adela's cheek. I walk over to Sophia and gently place my hand on her shoulder.

Doc Thierman motions to me. We walk out of the room. "Doc, how is she doing?" I ask.

"Adela isn't doing well. She has been coughing for several

weeks but she hadn't said anything. She told me that she thought that it was just a cold. Adela came to me when she began coughing blood. I've seen this before. There is nothing that I or anyone else can do to help her. You and Sophia need to prepare yourselves. I'm afraid that Adela will be passing soon. Adela has no family that I know of. You two are the closest thing she has to a family. Johann, I'm going to be leaving now, you know how to reach me when you need me. I'll give her something to help her sleep. Johann, the best thing that you can do for her, is, to be honest with her."

Adela passed away quietly, late in the evening. Sophia lost a dear friend. Adela is the closest thing to a mother that Sophia ever knew.

Sophia has been working exceptionally hard since Adela died. It seems that it is her way of keeping her mind off of the loss of her friend. Or perhaps it's her way of building Adela's legacy.

Daniel stopped by today and offered to buy Sophia and Adela's sawmill. He wants to move it up to his logging property and put it on Fish Creek. He offered Sophia a generous price. After Sophia and I talked about it she accepted his offer. Sophia now owns the brewery and grist mill. All the other businesses are now sold.

I'm working at Daniel's logging site with the new foreman that I hired. He doesn't have any experience in the logging business. He was a foreman at a farming compound near Hamburg and I think that he knows how to manage work crews.

It's the end of the workday, so I ride over to Lake Michigan. I tie up old Bootsie and walk forty feet to the edge of the lake bluff and find a stump to sit on. It's relaxing sitting here, looking over the water, and listening to the seagulls. I hear my horse acting spooky. I think to myself, that must be one of the loggers coming over here for something. Bootsie now sounds like she's panicking. I swing around to see that five enormous wolves have encircled my mare. They are getting ready to move in for the kill. As I turn, the wolves see me. Three of them run away for a short distance and stop. The bigger two, hold their ground. The other three then return to their positions. The wolves are moving in closer to Bootsie. My musket is in the scabbard that's on Bootsie. I'm looking around for a weapon. There's nothing but branches that were trimmed from the trees that we cut down. Those wolves are smart. They know that my mare is unable to run away and is easy prey for them. They are keeping an eye on me as well. They know that they have me outnumbered. I haven't made an offensive move toward them so now they aren't seeing me as a threat. It seems that the wolves are seeing me as their competition in killing the horse and they are prepared to fight me for her.

I can see that the only way I'll survive this stand off with the wolves is to surrender my mare to them and withdraw. I pick up a tree branch and I back up slowly with my eyes on the wolves. I sense that the wolves are more interested in my mare than they are in me. As I'm backing up, I can hear the wolves growling as they move in on my mare. Old Bootsie knows that I'm betraying her. When I get far enough away from the wolves, I turn and walk forward to the mess hall. The wolves are out of sight now, but I can hear the wolves attacking and pulling down my mare.

There are a couple of painful yelps coming from the wolves indicating to me that Bootsie contacted with her kicks. I'll miss Bootsie. That old mare served me well.

"Bootsie, you may have saved my life tonight."

With that thought, the wolves begin howling. Wolves will howl to announce a kill. I'm walking back to the mess hall at our logger's camp and it's getting dark. I have at least a quarter mile left to walk. I'm thinking of a conversation that I had with Des Bois. He is the hunter that I hired to shoot deer and elk for camp meat. He was telling me that the heavy snows and very cold temperatures that we have had this winter, killed a lot of deer and elk that the wolves depend on for their food. The starving wolf packs have been forced to hunt closer to human populations than they normally do. He said that wolves rarely attack humans.

But he knows of an Indian squaw that had been killed and eaten by wolves in this area last week.

I arrive at the mess hall and eat dinner. It's too late to ride home tonight so I'll spend the night here in the mess hall. I'll ride one of the company horses home tomorrow morning. I know that Sophia will be worrying about me, and it troubles me. One of the employees benefits that we offer to our loggers is that there will be a keg of beer and a hot meal waiting for them at the end of each workday. We have a great group of men working for us. After dinner and a pint or to of beer, we are telling stories and jokes.

The men call our camp, Mequon. One of our men belongs to the Potawatomi Indian tribe. His family lives in a village that is about five miles Northwest of our logging camp. He told us that his village is located at a place where the Mequonsippi Creek (white men call it Pigeon Creek) meets the Milwaukee River. The Potawatomi call the village that is located there, Mequon. I guess the loggers liked the name and began using it as the camp's name.

Chapter Sixteen

Home Sweet Homestead

I arrive back in Milwaukee at around 9:00 in the morning to find Sophia working at her grist mill. I can see that she is really angry. One of the millers didn't show up today, and they're behind on their orders. Also, one her brewers at the brewery quit and went to work for her competitor, Byron Kilbourn.

I don't know why I think that this is a good time to tell her about the land that I found up in Mequon. "Darling, do you have a moment?" She looks up. With sweat running down her face, she snaps back, "A moment? Do I have a Damn moment? Does It look like I have a moment?"

I quietly answer in a fearful voice, "Well...kind of. There's a pause. We both break out laughing. She walks over to me, hugs me, and gives me a kiss on my cheek, and then a punch in my arm.

She asks, "Well, where the Hell were you last night? You had me worried all night. I couldn't sleep!"

I respond, "I'll explain in a moment dear. Sophia, let's step outside and get away from this noise."

We go out and sit down on a bench near the mill stream, where I tell her about the land in Mequon. She pauses and stares at me with an empty expression, then looks down as she is choosing her words. I'm bracing to get blasted again.

Sophia looks up into my eyes and says, "Johann, the Lord

introduced you to me in a dark stable. It was the darkest time of my life. I was praying to God, asking to be saved from my father. At that moment, you appeared in front of me. I was afraid. He told me not to fear you and to trust you. He told me to follow you. Before that moment, I had learned to trust no one. I followed you across oceans and across continents. At some point in our journey to Milwaukee, I fell in love with you. I had never known love until that moment. I had never loved, and I had never been loved. I trust in God, and I trust in you. I believe that our Lord has shown you our final home. It will be the place that we are going to have our children and raise our family. We will live there for the rest of our lives."

I pause while I'm processing what Sophia has said. How did I get so blessed to have found this woman? I stand up in front of her, reach to her and hold both of her hands.

I ask, "Are you sure that you want to leave our home, our neighbors, and your businesses?"

Sophia replies, "The businesses aren't the same without Adela running them with me. It used to enjoy working with her. It's just not fun anymore. A while back Daniel asked me if I would be interested in selling the brewery. I'll let him know that the grist mill is available too."

I respond, "Are you sure that's what you want to do? I haven't talked to Daniel about buying his land yet. I was waiting to talk to you first. If you like, I'll talk to him today."

When I talk to Daniel, he says that the land in Mequon is available for sale. It is at a fair price, so I told him that I'll buy it. We want to include Sophia in our negotiation, so Daniel and I go over to her brewery where she's working. Daniel offers to trade 34 acres of the lake property that I want in exchange for Sophia's brewery. He also makes a cash offer for her grist mill.

We will close on the deal after the land is logged. Weather permitting, the closing will be on July first. We put the deal in writing then sign and date it. The three of us have a freshly brewed mug of beer to seal the deal. *Daniel Wells Jr.*

On July 2, 1831, Sophia and I begin building our log home on our new homestead. The logging crew heard about what we are doing, and they come over after work to help us. Daniel had the lumber cut for the door and window framing at his sawmill and had it delivered to our new house. He said it is a housewarming gift. Our new house is built in two weeks.

Loggers had cut down and removed all the big trees that were on our land before we purchased it. Sophia and I are working every day from sunup to sundown clearing the small trees and stumps that were left by the loggers. By the end of November, we have cleared about two acres of land. We will be able to plant wheat, corn, and vegetables on the land in spring.

The year after Sophia and I bought our land, Daniel began selling the rest of his land that had been logged to other settlers. Most of our new neighbors have arrived from German-speaking countries. We also have a few Irishmen and Yankees homesteading nearby too.

Fruition

Today I'm celebrating my 89th birthday with Sophia, our three sons, three daughters and nine grandchildren.

Reflecting back over the years. I've been blessed to have been able to fulfill my dream. Sophia and I own our own farm in Mequon.

I remember when we planted our first crop in 1831, on the first two acres that we had cleared. We continued clearing our land every day until our land was completely tillable in 1835.

Sophia and I have six children. They were all born and raised here on our farm.

Maria is our first born. We named her after her grandmother. She married her childhood sweetheart, Otis Kiefer that lived up the road. Sadly, we lost our second and third children, Ida, and Fritz at the age of one and three to chicken pox. It broke Sophia's heart and she has never completely recovered from our loss.

Louis is our fourth child. Tragically, he lost his wife, Sara, during childbirth. The baby named Katherine survived. Louis never remarried. Little Katherine, I call her Katie, liked to ride along with me when I would go to Johann Thien's Mill. After attending to business, I used to like to have a pint of ale or two at August Riemer's saloon called "The Commercial House." Katie would play with August's little boy named, Alvin while I was attending to business at the mill. Katie ended up marrying Alvin.

Next in line are our twins, Petrus, named in honor of his grandfather and Anna, we named her after my sister. Anna never married. She died in 1845 and is buried next to our dear little Ida at the Opitz Cemetery. Petrus married Anna Barth. They have five children. Petrous and Anna have a fifty six-acre farm nearby on Lake Shore Road.

~~John Jr. is our youngest. He married Se~~lma Haentz. Selma died in 1858. John and Selma have one surviving child named Johnny. John has a forty-acre farm on Mequon Road.

I never heard from my brothers Otto and Dietrich since the day they went off to fight in the Creek War years ago. I always looked up to them and I still do. I have given up hope that they are still alive. I am still so proud of them, and I miss them terribly.

We haven't seen my sister Anna, her since the time she came to Milwaukee for our attempted wedding seventy-one years ago. Anna writes to Sophia and I from time to time. The Captain sold his steamship many years ago, and bought into an international shipping company based in Baltimore.

As for Sophia, well, she still has that flirtatious giggle that I fell in love with sixty-three years ago when we were just sixteen years old. That brass ring that I gave her on the day that I asked her to be my wife is still on her left hand. As you probably guessed, I'm still getting punched in the arm on occasion.

Sophia and I never did get around to getting married. She accepted my name on our wedding day and has been known to everyone as Mrs. Johann Kemp ever since. We've talked about having our wedding from time to time, but never did get around to it. I guess we were too busy running the farm and raising our children to take a day off for a wedding.

Sophia Kemp
Died 1892

Johann Kemp
Died 1890

Johann and Sophia died peacefully of natural causes on Their farm. They are buried side by side in the Opitz Cemetery in Mequon, Wisconsin.

A Final Thought

I'm speaking with humble gratitude as Johann and Sophia's seventy-two-year-old great-great grandson.

I can only imagine how hard it was for Johann and Sophia living on the American frontier during the nineteenth century. But, as hard as life was for them, it was far better than the life of servitude that Johann left behind in Mecklenburg.

I have on occasion, thought of Johann's cousins who chose to stay in their hopeless situation in Mecklenburg. Unlike Johann, they didn't have the vision to see themselves in a better place. Or perhaps, they didn't have the courage to leave the place that their families had lived for generations.

My ancestors who chose to stay in Mecklenburg suffered the hardship of World War I and the bombings of World War II. In the final weeks of WWII, my Riemer and Kemp relatives experienced rampant rape and murder perpetrated by the Russian Army during their invasion of Germany.

After WWII the Allied countries divided Germany into two parts. One part had a democratic government, and the other had a communist government. The Provence of Mecklenburg was in the Communist part. My relatives suffered living under the totalitarian Communist East German government rule for forty-one years until the German reunification in 1990.

Thank you, Johann, and Sophia, for your courage and all that you had risked so that my family and I could live free and prosper as Americans!

The End

Cast of Characters

Johann Kemp	Age sixteen years old
Anna Kemp	Johann's sister, age fifteen years old
Grandfather	Johann's grandfather, Grubvater in German
Grandmother	Johann's grandmother, Grubmutter in German
Petrus Kemp	Johann's father, Voter in German
Maria Kemp	Johann's mother, Mutter in German
Dietrich Kemp	Johann's older brother
Otto Kemp	Johann's older brother
Baron Von Gutenriemer	Sophia's father, Nobleman landowner
Sophia Gutenriemer	The Baron's daughter, age sixteen years old
Caption McCarthy	Anna's husband
Hans and Anita	Traveled with the group to Pittsburgh Parents of Rudy, Heidi, and Olga
Fritz	Traveled with the group to Pittsburgh
Nitkuxkwike	Member of the Lenni Lenape tribe Born to English settlers.
Abraham	Retired American Army sergeant traveling with Johann to Fort Dearborn.

George Walker	Johann's friend, lived on the south side of Milwaukee.
Solomon Juneau	Johann's friend and employer
Josette Juneau	Solomon Juneau's wife
General Hull	Commanding General at Fort Dearborn
Jamie (JT) Smith	Constable in Milwaukee
Byron Kilbourn	Land developer on the west side of the river in Milwaukee
Adela Firean	Sophia's business partner
Daniel Wells Jr.	Johann's friend and employer in Milwaukee
Millie Wells	Daniel's wife, her father calls her Millicent
Baron Von Voght	First name Casper, father of Millie Wells
Brutus	Baron Von Gutenriemer's bodyguard
Cornelius Smith	JT Smith's brother
Allen Lapam	Employed by Byron Kilbourn
Garret Veliet	Employed by Byron Kilbourn.

Kemp family farms in 1880
Town of Mequon, Wisconsin

JOHANN AND SOPHIA'S
ORIGINAL HOMESTEAD IN 1831

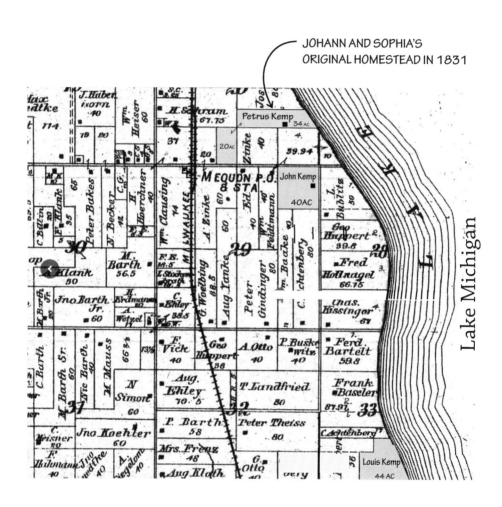

Kemp family members. Photo taken behind the first Thiensville dam in about 1910. Back row left to right, Olga Kemp Gramoll, Elizabeth Kemp, Rosa Kemp, Unknown, Sophia Kemp (not Johann's wife) Anna Barth Kemp. Front row, Unknown, Unknown, Lilla Gramoll, Chester Gramoll, Orville Gramoll.

Johann & Sophia Kemp's
original homestead location overlaid on an
aerial photograph of Mequon, Wisconsin

Google Earth satellite photograph taken in 2021

About the Author

Richard Riemer is a great-great-great grandson of this story's hero and heroine, Johann and Sophia Kemp. Richard's grandmother is Johann's great-grand daughter, Katherine (Katie) Kemp. Katie married Richard's grand father, Alvin Riemer in 1907. Richard has studied the  Riemer and Kemp family history all of his life. He recently wrote a documentary about Johann and Sophia's descendants titled "The Riemer and Kemp Story."

Richard was a resident of Thiensville and Mequon Wisconsin for twenty-six years. He then lived in the neighboring town of Grafton. Richard now resides in Scottsdale, Arizona.

Books may be purchased through Amazon.

email: rick.l.riemer@gmail.com

Made in the USA
Monee, IL
14 September 2022